The Vermont Gambit

A NOVEL OF ALTERNATE HISTORY

LARRY CHIGER

ISBN 979-8-9922953-2-0 (Paperback)
ISBN 979-8-9922953-3-7 (eBook)

Visit the author's website:
www.larrychigerauthor.com

Cover design by Miblart: www.miblart.com

For my family: my wife Maria, my children Nathan and Rebecca, and their spouses Julie and Jake

Contents

Preface

This story continues the alternate timeline I established in *For Our Cause Was Just*, where the American Revolution failed before France's official entry into the war.

The following excerpt, written in the form of a personal memoir, provides background on how this world diverged from our own history. Readers of the previous novel will recognize the last paragraph from the epilogue of that book.

Excerpt from *Observations from the Late Rebellion in Nor. America*, 1784, Patrick Ferguson

Thus concludes my account of the surrender of the Continental Army in the late rebellion in Nor. America beginning with the Engagement near Brandywine Creek and ending in Philadelphia. My chance encounter with General George Washington, Commander of the rebel Army days prior to our attack that Sept. 1777, resulting in his capture and death, did set in motion a course of reunification of the British Empire under King George III.

I had desired to take Gen. Washington and his companion prisoners rather than fire upon them from hiding. Alas, it was not to be; after I stepped into view and demanded their surrender an errant shot from one of my men rang out and Washington fell. While we tended to the wounded Man as best we could, and returned with him to our camp surgeon, his Wound proved mortal.

I later learned from prisoners that the News of General Washington's Death spread through the American Lines with the Swiftness of Lightning, & the Effect upon their Troops was most Remarkable. Their will broken, our victory and occupation of their capital Philadelphia was inevitable. While the rebels clung to hope, their Congress negotiated the conclusion of the rebellion after the severe Winter of 1777-78. Though our Victory was complete, I shall always carry the Weight of that Moment.

His Majesty, upon receiving Word of these Events, did show the greatest Magnanimity in Victory. Rather than impose harsh Punishments upon the rebellious Colonies, the King in his Wisdom established a Continental Council, granting to the Americans representation in Parliament & a Voice in the governing of their own Affairs. Thus was the Rebellion brought to its End, not through Severity, but through the gracious Mercy of our Sovereign.

I have to believe that if circumstances had been reversed, and my rifleman had not fired that fateful shot, we would have prevailed nonetheless. For our cause was just, and I cannot imagine that God in heaven above would have ordained any other result than to bring our brothers back to the fold of their gracious King.

Prologue

The crunch of his steps on the early-morning frozen earth echoed in his ears. Elias Armistead and his fellow Green Mountain Rangers pursued the New York militia—men who until recently had been their allies. But now, Vermont fought for its independence, and Elias fought to protect his home, his wife, and their unborn child. Nathaniel Reed kept pace beside him, musket in hand.

"I don't like this, Nathaniel," Elias whispered. "They've got horse-men with them. What does the colonel think we're going to do against horsemen?"

"I'm sure he has a plan. Our unit has held our own in every skirmish we've had. This one will be no different—if we find them."

"The sooner this is over, the better. I want to get back home to Lucy," Elias continued. "Ever since she told me she's with child, I cannot think of anything else but being with her."

"I'm happy for you," Nathaniel spoke softly. "And I know Lucy will be a fine mother. You married into a great family." He flashed a smile at Elias and gave him a playful shove.

The colonel raised his arm, signaling them to halt at the brook along the forest's edge. Beyond it, a meadow stretched wide before giving way to another line of trees—open ground that would no longer conceal their presence. He unfastened the leather case at his side and drew out a spyglass, lifting it to his eye. A flash of movement caught his attention—the shifting of shadowy figures among the pines. And then the riders emerged.

"We've been spotted!" Colonel Fairbanks cried. "There's six—no, wait, two more—eight horsemen coming toward us." *Eight horsemen against my twenty men,* he thought. *We can take them—if we have a better defensive position.* "The stone wall on the far side of the woods!" he shouted. "At the double! I want a firing line behind that wall we passed!"

It was challenging to hold the men together as they scrambled through the brush, his orders becoming lost amongst the trees. Some of his men heard him. Others were out of range or could not hear above the sound of their own footfalls landing hard as they ran. Then came the sound of horses crashing into the wood.

Elias ran as fast as he could. A stumble in the underbrush threw him to the ground. Picking up his musket, he righted himself. He had lost sight of his comrade-in-arms. *Bloody hell.* He heard the horses somewhere behind him. He crouched in the frozen mud, peering around a maple tree's rough bark, knowing his pursuers could be upon him at any moment. The sound of the horses reached him before he saw them. He leveled his musket at the charging horse, his right index finger on the trigger. The horseman grew closer. Elias squeezed the trigger. A flash. The shot rang out, but the charging figure rode on. He fumbled with the musket, his back pressed against the maple, his fingers numb with cold. Before he reloaded, the soldier returned at a charge. Elias barely ducked in time, the sword slicing the air above him.

I could have killed him had I been loaded, Elias thought. He finished loading his musket and replaced the ramrod.

Without warning, the rider reappeared, slashing at him with his sword, just missing him again as he rode by. Elias lost his balance. His elbow hit the ground, dislodging his musket from his hand. The mounted swordsman rounded a pine tree. On his knees, Elias grabbed his musket. The soldier bore down on him. Elias fired.

The horseman twisted in his saddle and fell from his steed. Elias relaxed, but only for a scant few seconds, tensing again as the soldier rose to his feet, sword in hand. His spent musket useless, a surge of panic rose within him. Instinct took over; he jumped up and gripped the musket like a club. The soldier charged toward Elias, his sword outstretched. Elias took a defensive position, ready to use his musket to block the expected slash. He flinched at the crack of a musket shot. The soldier fell dead at Elias's feet, blood draining from the hole in the back of his head. He turned to see Nathaniel Reed, calm and focused, reloading his musket.

"I owe you for that," Elias stammered, reloading his musket.

"There's more of them," Nathaniel muttered. "And we've fallen behind."

Elias and Nathaniel moved forward, muskets cocked, each footstep announcing their presence. They made their way through the brush and around the trees. Elias led, with Nathaniel close at his back, watching behind them as they made their way. Elias abruptly stopped. In front of him lay a green-coated ranger face down, the wound to the back of his shoulder leaving a rusty stain. Elias turned the body over.

"Nothing we can do for him now, damn them," Elias grumbled. "We need to keep moving."

They continued to make their way through the forest, attempting to catch up with their unit. Elias heard it first: the sound of hoofbeats racing toward them, but this time from in front of them. They had been spotted. A rider charged forward. Elias knelt on one knee on the frozen soil and peered down his musket barrel. Nathaniel stood over him, also with his musket aimed.

"I'll take this one," Nathaniel said, then fired. But the soldier continued forward.

They ran. Elias heard the horse gaining on him. A slip on the frozen ground threw him to his back, and he felt the whoosh of a slashing blade through the space he just vacated. The horseman then chased Nathaniel with his sword raised. From the cold earth, Elias pointed his musket and fired. The sword dropped from the soldier's hand, allowing Nathaniel to escape around a tree. Wheeling his steed to face Elias, the mounted soldier drew a pistol. Elias scrambled to his feet just as the horseman fired. Elias clutched at his chest, his face fixed in disbelief. Lucy's face flared before him—her eyes bright as she told him of their child. It was the last image he ever saw.

"No!" Nathaniel screamed, his face red with anger. He fired his reloaded musket. The soldier tumbled from his horse, unmoving.

Chapter 1

The Best-Laid Schemes

The Boston office of the general of the Northern Continental Army, Horatio Gates, was as Baron Friedrich Wilhelm von Steuben remembered it. Only this time, the fireplace glowed with an ethereal green light that provided no heat. He shivered. The mahogany bookshelves that once held dusty leather-bound tomes now contained fish leaping from shelf to shelf. He blinked. The general's image flickered like a candle flame as he stared at him.

The baron's interpreter, Pierre Etienne du Ponceau, stood silently beside him, the green fire highlighting his wavy copper hair, his dark eyes fixed on the baron. Though Pierre was only seventeen, the baron felt comforted by his steady presence, his sharp mind making him a valued aide.

"We are no longer in need of your services," Gates said, his face stern. Pierre translated for the baron as Gates spoke.

The baron's jaw dropped, but no words came out. Finally, he uttered one word in English. "Why?"

"For conduct unbecoming an officer," Gates snapped.

"What conduct? I've done nothing but improve our force. They are better prepared now for battle against the British, yet there is still more to do."

"I don't need to provide a reason."

"I demand it!"

"You are in no position to demand anything! My reasons are my reasons. That is all you need to know. You're dismissed." Gates picked up correspondence from the table before him and pretended to read it.

As he stood there, his feet refusing to move, the faint sound of waves that should not have been there reached the baron's ears. He turned to where the sound came from, then back to Gates. His heart raced as the room blurred, the scent of saltwater filling his nostrils, and the sound of waves growing louder until Gates's visage dissolved into the mast of a ship. The baron was now on the deck and holding onto the rail as a wave crashed over, a bitter wind lashed at him, and rain pelted his face. The captain's orders screamed, barely audible over the roar of the angry North Atlantic winter. Pierre arrived beside him, and the baron saw fear in his eyes. *Mach dir keine Sorgen—don't worry*—he wanted to shout at Pierre, but before he could get the words out, a rogue wave crashed over the ship and swept Pierre over the side.

"*Nein!*" the baron yelled as he startled awake, grabbing at the air.

Pierre bolted upright beside him. "Is it the nightmare again?"

"Yes, but this time..." He buried his head in his hands.

"You don't need to fret about another winter crossing of the Atlantic. It's better we decided to seek out Congress instead," Pierre said.

"All that time working with Generals Gates and Hancock, just to have John Hancock turn on us and throw us out of his home."

"I think he found out about our relationship," Pierre said, searching his features in the dark. "You know how people are. That's why we have to keep it secret."

"I still don't understand it." The baron shook his head, trying to rid Gate's voice from his mind. "I impressed General Gates—impressed enough to appoint me inspector general. The army's training was progressing; they were using the new manual of drills I wrote. The men were skilled. Better disciplined. I'm sure they would have matched the British come spring. Now?"

"The sooner we make it to Congress in Pennsylvania, the better." Pierre's voice softened as he slipped his arm around him. "Lie back down."

The baron and du Ponceau's journey was taking longer than expected. Days before, while traveling through Massachusetts, they deviated north along the Connecticut River to avoid British patrols. Their trek across what they believed were the Berkshire Mountains proved to be more difficult than anticipated, based on the information they had obtained in Boston. The late afternoon winter sun bathed the fields in golden rays, shimmering off the white frozen landscape.

Cold and tired, the baron was dreading another night in a tent with only their dried rations to eat when he noticed smoke in the distance. He hoped they would find a welcoming home where he and du Ponceau could find a brief respite from the freezing weather. They rode on following the icy dirt road and crested a small ridge. A hamlet emerged; they could see a cluster of homes and the steeple of a church. They rode into the small town.

A man bundled within a cloak, a three-cornered cocked hat pulled down, hurried along the road, his head bent low to fend off the wind whipping across the open fields. As they approached him, du Ponceau called out, "Good sir!" The man did not hear him as a sudden gust of wind carried his words away. "Good sir!" he yelled louder. The man stopped, turned to the unexpected voice, and stared at the two men on their horses. "Good evening," said du Ponceau, who usually spoke for the baron. Though von Steuben had learned some English while he trained the Continental troops, most were swear words. "Could you tell us if there is an inn in this village for two weary travelers?"

"You're in luck," the man replied, pointing at a two-story white building with a red gambrel roof. "That's the Dewey Tavern. I'm sure they have room. We don't get many strangers this time of year."

"Thank you kindly."

They rode the half-mile to the tavern. Though they now knew the inn's name, they were still unaware of where they were. Du Ponceau dismounted, and the baron took hold of his horse's reins while du Ponceau went inside. He was gone just a few minutes before reappearing looking anxious.

"I've secured a room for the night. Someone will be along in a few minutes for our horses."

"*Gut!* So why the look of concern?" von Steuben asked.

"We're in Bennington in the Vermont Republic."

The Vermont Republic was neither British nor American. It had declared independence from New York in early 1777 and fiercely defended it. Because it was officially neutral in the war between Great Britain and the nascent United States, the republic became a haven for deserters from both armies. However, skirmishes with the New York militia were a common occurrence. The baron had wanted to avoid traveling through the Vermont Republic, but they would have to make the best of it now that they were here.

A stable hand materialized, but before he could whisk their weary steeds away for care and feeding, the baron removed a large leather satchel attached to the saddle. As he did so, a small jet-black head popped out of the pouch. The baron petted his ever-present companion, Azor, an Italian greyhound, nestled in his fleece-lined confines.

The creak of the tavern door announced the arrival of the baron, du Ponceau, and Azor, still in his bag. Stepping inside, they found the small common room surprisingly bustling. More men than they'd anticipated for such a quiet hamlet filled the space—at least twenty, possibly more.

A massive stone fireplace roared at the far end, radiating warmth that battled the chill clinging to them. Wrought-iron sconces, each boasting three flickering candles, cast a warm glow on the scene. The baron removed his beaver fur hat, wiped his boots on the mud-caked wool mats by the entrance, and ventured onto the rough wooden floorboards. As they navigated toward an empty table, the lively chatter dipped noticeably. Eyes followed the newcomers, assessing their presence. Both wore Continental blue coats with white facings, but that's where any resemblance stopped. The two presented a stark contrast—the baron's stout figure and du Ponceau's slight frame.

Claiming a worn pine table with an equally weathered bench, they settled in. Conversations gradually resumed, unspoken acceptance settling over the room as the patrons deemed them no immediate danger.

The baron scanned his surroundings. Several men sported military uniforms unlike any he'd ever encountered. The shade of deep-summer sugar maple leaves, this forest green echoed the hue of the Vermont Republic's flag and contrasted with crisp cardinal red facings.

They wore tan buckskin waistcoats over checkered black-and-white shirts, which were tucked into breeches made of the same material as the waistcoats.

Some men sported black boots cut just below the knee, while others had rough white knee-high wool socks and sturdy leather shoes. Black felt tricornes hung on wall hooks, perched atop stained and faded hunting frocks. A collection of muskets—English, French, and likely American—leaned against the wall, keeping silent company with the hats.

A barmaid, the only woman in the tavern, appeared at the baron's side. Du Ponceau, acting as translator, queried her about the available fare. He settled on chicken pot pie, buttermilk biscuits, and local ale for them both. The ale arrived swiftly, quenching their thirst while they awaited the main course.

"Seems there's more military movement about than I anticipated," the baron murmured in hushed German. "Yet they don't appear worried by outsiders."

The barmaid returned bearing steaming pot pies, fluffy biscuits, and a pair of forks. The baron broke off a biscuit piece, holding it to the small black head peeking from the satchel beside him. Azor snatched it eagerly. "I'll get more than just biscuits for you, my friend," the baron chuckled, gazing down at his canine companion. "Pierre, flag down the barmaid. Perhaps they have some chicken scraps they could cook for Azor?"

With a satisfied sigh, the baron dug into the pot pie. He navigated the potatoes, carrots, and onions with his fork, finally extracting a juicy piece of chicken. He relished the taste, discarding the bones onto the tabletop. The warm, savory dish was a welcome change from the cold rations they'd endured for the last week.

They settled in and enjoyed their meal amid the clatter of cutlery and the low murmur of conversation. Azor, ever vigilant, watched as the barmaid brought a plate of chicken liver and other giblets. The baron fed it by hand to the eagerly awaiting dog. Then the tavern door swung open, a blast of frigid air whipping around their legs.

Three figures entered: two men—one clad in a forest green uniform like the others, one in civilian clothing—and a woman. As the woman shouldered the door shut, a chorus of greetings erupted: "General!" and "Ira!" The men in the tavern roared their welcomes.

The baron's gaze snagged on the lead figure, whose forest green regimental boasted insignia that marked him as an officer. A tall man, perhaps a decade younger than the baron's forty-seven years, with a keen face and sharp nose; his thin lips formed an easy smile. He moved with practiced ease, his laughter echoing as he greeted patrons. Firm handshakes were exchanged, backs slapped in camaraderie.

The second man, younger by another ten years or so, unbuttoned a dark gray greatcoat to reveal a more formal ensemble: a dark blue coat, tan waistcoat, and brown breeches. With a round face and a hooked nose under wide-set brown eyes, he kept his voice low in conversation as he followed the boisterous officer.

Last came the woman. The tavern light made her age unclear, possibly a bit younger than the civilian. Her demeanor held a curious mix of weariness and quiet determination. Under her cloak, a simple gray wool dress clung to her thin form, its plainness accentuated by a checkered apron devoid of frills. A white kerchief, unable to fully contain unruly auburn hair, was tied around her head. Her hazel eyes, with flecks of green and gold, shimmered as she passed the candlelight.

She offered no smiles, her expression unreadable as she navigated the boisterous room. Unlike the men beside her, she remained silent, a stark contrast to the jovial greetings that surrounded them.

The officer spotted the strangers first. He and a few patrons exchanged words while heads turned to the baron and his companion. Several men shook their heads in response to a question that didn't reach the baron's ears. The officer conferred with his civilian acquaintance before they approached the baron, the woman trailing behind them.

"Brigadier General Seth Warner, Vermont Republic, at your service, sir." He extended a hand to the baron in greeting. "This is my cousin, Ira Allen."

The baron grasped Warner's hand, but his gaze shifted to his translator. Du Ponceau bridged the language gap with German.

"German?" Warner said with a tinge of wariness. "Are you Hessian?"

The baron understood this, and he quickly said, "No!" Then, in German to du Ponceau, "In Portsmouth, they thought we were British; here they think we're damned Hessians." The baron rose to his feet, a respectable height but not quite matching Warner's stature. "I am Baron Friedrich Wilhelm von Steuben," he said. He gestured to his companion. "And this is Pierre Etienne du Ponceau."

Warner's face flashed with surprise once more, but he quickly replaced it with a smile. "May we join you?"

The baron simply said, "Yes," pointing at the bench. Warner and Allen sat down, the woman taking a seat across the table.

"Gentleman, allow me to introduce my sister, Mrs. Armistead," Allen said.

The two men nodded their hellos as du Ponceau briefly explained to the group that the baron spoke limited English and his role as translator. The barmaid interrupted the introduction as she arrived with three bowls of venison stew.

"It's good to see you again, General. You too, Mr. Allen. I've brought your favorite. I'll be back with your ale. Lucy, I hope you're doing better." Without waiting for a response, she was off again.

"We heard of your presence in Boston, aiding the Continental troops," Warner said. "What brings you to our humble corner of the world?"

"A lot has changed since my arrival on these shores," von Steuben responded through du Ponceau. He spoke of his letter of introduction to George Washington, written by Benjamin Franklin, which he still retained. "Only after we arrived did we learn of George Washington's death and the Southern Army's surrender. With the general dead, everything fell apart." He shook his head, still in disbelief.

Warner glanced down at his hands before returning his gaze to von Steuben. "The papers say he was ambushed. Congress hanged the spy responsible, but the damage was done. Without Washington, the army had no chance at Brandywine." He looked off in the distance, momentarily lost in memory. "I fought alongside them not long ago."

"General Gates asked me to join his Northern Army as inspector general," the baron continued. "But now there's word that Congress is negotiating with the British, as I'm sure you've heard."

Warner scooped a spoonful of stew, but now paused, spoon in hand. "I know of rumors. You have details?"

"Heated discussions arose among his commanders concerning what course of action should be taken." Then von Steuben added a lie:

"Let's just say I found myself in disagreement with their plans and decided to seek new pastures."

"Those rumored negotiations were discussed at the Vermont Council today."

"My cousin here was promoted to brigadier general by the council," Allen interjected.

Warner shot Allen an annoyed look before turning back to the baron. "As I was saying, the discussion centered around the impact that would have on our republic." He took a deep draft of his ale. "It pained me deeply when I learned of the general's death. I never had the opportunity to meet him, but I know many who did. The respect they had for him is evident. Washington inspired his men and forced the British to respect his army's capabilities." He grimaced. "Now, what's left of that army frustrates me. The British have been too busy fighting that uprising to worry about this little corner of the world. But if Congress capitulates, they'll have the manpower and time to come for us next."

"My intent when arriving on these shores was to offer my services to better train his soldiers," von Steuben said. "I was successful in improving General Gates's army. Now we're headed to Congress where I can do the same for the army there."

"What's left of it," Warner murmured. The baron winced, for it echoed his thoughts. "I'd ponder if there is much you could do for them, considering the state they're in. Unless you have some intelligence on the British that might be useful?"

"I know they are the best trained and equipped army on this continent," the baron answered. "The advantage they now maintain over the Continentals make them even more formidable. Where does that leave Vermont?"

"Steadfast in our independence."

"But a British victory isolates Vermont. And they'll want to bring you back into the Empire. If you intend independence, your people must be prepared for the long fight."

Lucy looked up from her bowl of stew, her eyes fixed on the baron but looking through him. "Come York or come Hampshire, come traitors or knaves, if ye rule o'er our land, ye shall rule o'er our graves."

Startled by Lucy's sudden rush of speech, he considered her for a moment. "I respect the enthusiasm, but it will take more than enthusiasm to succeed," the baron said. "Tell me, General, what goods do you export?"

"Mostly agricultural. Timber, corn, wheat, and the best damned syrup in the world."

"If they block your trade, ensure no imports, it will be difficult, General."

"Baron, we Vermonters are a fierce people, independent and free. We've fought New York for our freedoms and have no intention of giving them up. We believe in liberty and self-determination. Unlike our neighbors, our constitution prohibits the repugnant scourge of slavery. We cannot turn back. And I've been tasked with ensuring we're prepared—for whatever may come next."

The baron leaned forward, his jaw tightening. "In Boston, I witnessed men fighting in the name of liberty while keeping others enslaved. The contradiction bewilders me." He shook his head. "You Vermonters seem to understand what they do not."

The three men discussed military strategies and tactics throughout their dinner. Lucy stared into her bowl as she ate until she scraped the bottom. She then interrupted the conversation. "Ira, the hour grows late, and I am tired. I want to head home."

"Yes. I'll escort you, Lucy." Allen stood up and extended his hand to the baron. "It's been a pleasure to speak with you this evening." After they donned their coats, he took his sister's arm and walked her out of the tavern.

The baron watched them as they left. "Uncommon sight to see a woman in a tavern," the baron said. "Unless they're serving. She seems so... troubled."

Warner's expression grew somber. "Her husband fell to New York forces. Grief took their unborn child too. She's been in a melancholy state ever since. Ira's been caring for her, but nothing seems to pierce the veil. Poor soul."

The baron sighed. "May she find solace soon. A spark of fire still burns within her, I saw that much."

"Indeed," Warner agreed, his voice heavy. "A firebrand she was before this war dimmed her spirit. I pray she reclaims that strength. Youth is still on her side." He sent the baron an inquiring look. "Perhaps with someone who understands the cost of such loss."

A chuckle escaped the baron. "Alas, I'm entangled elsewhere." He cast a passing glance at Pierre. "Let's hope Mr. Allen can reach her." He took a sip from his mug. "Now tell me, General, how would you deploy your forces if the Continentals succumb?"

Their conversation stretched far into the night, leaving them the sole patrons in the tavern. Finally, Warner leaned in, his voice low and serious. "Baron, your military expertise is undeniable. The path that led you here may have been circuitous, but I'm grateful for this chance encounter. The task ahead for our republic is monumental. We could use a man of your caliber. Will you stand with us in the fight for freedom?"

The baron met his gaze, a moment of indecision crossing his features. "Your offer is an honor, sir. It warrants careful consideration."

"Take your time." Warner rose. "We can resume this conversation tomorrow. Until then, good night." He shook the baron's hand firmly and exited the tavern.

"You're not seriously considering this, are you?" du Ponceau asked.

"If the American Congress negotiates a surrender to the British, where would that leave us? Perhaps this republic is what we need."

Chapter 2

Invitation

Captain Theodore Brehm sat hunched over his writing desk. Two lanterns burned close by. He tried to compose words of solace to his brother-in-law. Brehm had just received the letter informing him his younger sister died in childbirth, but his grief blocked his efforts. *It's almost as if it's a different lifetime*, he thought, burying his head in his hands, but the tears didn't come for the sister he remembered only as a child.

Brehm sighed, the weight of his personal loss clashing with his professional duty. *Perhaps work will help dull my grief*, he thought. Yet as he picked up the official correspondence, an image of his sister remained steadfast in his mind. He walked to the window and opened it higher, breathing in the night air.

Sitting again, he retrieved the letter he had begun writing to the Vermont Council for the new governor general of Quebec, Frederick Haldimand. Though only in his early thirties, Brehm was a trusted advisor and had been Haldimand's aide-de-camp for his recent North American assignments. He concentrated on the task before him: ensuring Vermont's reunification with the British Empire. Haldimand's priorities were clear—control the access routes from Lake Champlain and the Richelieu River from the lake to Montreal. Although the

Continentals had ended their rebellion, Vermont's control of the eastern shore of Lake Champlain remained a thorn in their side. Vermont's territory was vital to Quebec's defense, and his job was to get them to the negotiating table.

Brehm stared at what he had already written. *How do I phrase this so that they join talks and do not feel they're walking into a trap?* A summer breeze flowed through the open window, ruffling the papers on his desk. He placed a paperweight on the pages and continued writing.

> Therefore, we invite you to attend a conference here to discuss the grievances over New York that you previously presented to Gen. Clinton. We aim to forge a way forward in peace now that the late rebellion in N. America is over. I have enclosed a letter of invitation that will allow entry to Upper Town Quebec City and provide you with safe passage. The presence of your representatives would honour us.

He closed with a valediction and signed Haldimand's name. Brehm reread the invitation and placed it aside. He wrote the letter of invitation providing entry to Quebec, enclosed it in his letter, and secured it with a wax seal. The following day, it would go out by ship to New York and from there to Bennington.

Brehm once again stared at the letter from his brother-in-law. *How can mere words be of any solace?* But that was all he had to offer. He wiped a tear from his cheek.

Dear Alfred,

The grievous news of Elizabeth's death has reached me.

The words flowed from his quill.

———————•◦•———————

A warm summer breeze rustled the maple leaves as General Warner stood beside the baron, now inspector general of the Vermont Republic's army. The two men stood together atop a rise overlooking a battalion of Green Mountain Rangers drilling, their maneuvers watched with an unflinching scrutiny by the baron. Von Steuben was not smiling. But he hardly ever smiled when training the men. He focused on hunting out any flaw that could spell defeat on the battlefield. General Warner, having grown to know the baron well over the past three months since that fortuitous encounter at the Dewey Tavern, had already learned this.

The baron, too, had benefited from their encounter. Had he continued his intended course to the American Congress, he would have arrived when the war's capitulation letters were signed—the formal end of the American rebellion. In the Vermont Republic, he found kindred spirits—a republic seeking freedom for all men. Their current challenge was building a formidable army to deter an invasion. So far, there had been no British incursions. However, the border with New York continued to erupt in skirmishes with their militia.

"What do you think?" Warner asked.

The baron grunted a sound that seemed to combine a growl and a curse of his native German. "Improved, but not yet adept in the new manual," du Ponceau translated. Von Steuben gestured vaguely toward the worn leather-bound book tucked under his arm. It was the drill manual he had painstakingly crafted, heavily influenced by the Prussian and Continental Army versions but adapted for Vermont's rugged, mountainous landscape.

"We acquitted ourselves well in those skirmishes with the Yorkers," Warner said.

The baron scoffed. "The Yorkers were merely townsfolk masquerading as militia."

"I daresay they weren't expecting such a well-drilled force," Warner responded, a swell of satisfaction in his chest. "The sight of them scrambling back across the river was glorious!" He caught the glimmer of a smile on the baron's face, as fleeting as the summer breeze, quickly replaced by a noncommittal grunt. "High praise from you! I'll take that."

"The British, should we fight them, will prove a far worthier opponent. There's much work to be done." The baron gave a curt shake of his head but let his lips curl into a small smile. "Ach, look at that formation. Will they ever get this right?" Even before du Ponceau finished translating, the baron was striding purposefully down the hill, Azor scampering beside him.

Warner watched him go with a sigh. The baron could be a gruff taskmaster, but his dedication to the Green Mountain Rangers was undeniable. A surge of pride filled Warner as he watched the flag fluttering in the breeze behind the troops—a rich forest-green field emblazoned with a canton of deep blue housing thirteen five-pointed stars arranged in a scattered constellation. Under the baron's harsh tutelage, his rangers had transformed over the past three months. Their ragged lines had tightened and their movements grown more purposeful, a testament to their newfound discipline.

As he watched, a shadow blocked the sun. He turned to find Ira Allen standing beside him with a wide grin.

"I didn't expect you out here today," Warner said.

"You've spoken so much about the improvement of our rangers, I wanted to see them for myself."

They stood and watched the baron barking orders below, pacing between unit commanders and directing them to maneuver their men more effectively. He soon had them deploying smoothly across the open field.

"They look good," Allen said. "And have performed well in these recent border skirmishes. I've read your written reports. But if the Yorkers get the backing of the British, with British troops..." His voice trailed off.

Warner knew Allen was right. The border skirmishes were a constant source of tension. While a full-blown British invasion didn't seem imminent, there was always the chance of escalation.

"The baron's preparing them," Warner said. "He wouldn't push them so hard if he didn't believe they could match them on the battlefield."

"It's the numbers that concern me. Now that the Continental Army has disbanded, there's no one to keep them occupied. And that's the other reason I came out to see you. I leave tomorrow for Quebec."

Ira Allen had been appointed a diplomat by the Vermont Council. He was to travel to Quebec City to negotiate with the new governor general of Quebec. His mission was to secure an agreement to halt the New York militia's raids.

"I'm not so sure the British are interested in reining in the Yorkers," Warner said, for he was aware of the task before Allen. "It likely serves them well to keep us in a constant state of unease. They know the more forces we must dedicate to the border, the fewer we maintain to defend against a full-scale incursion. It's a tricky path you walk, but I know you're up to the job."

"Thank you."

"And what of Lucy?" Warner asked.

"She will accompany me." Allen looked at the ground and shook his head before raising it and continuing, "I don't know, Seth. It's been a long while, and she hasn't returned to her former self; now I sometimes doubt she ever will. She perked up a bit as the days grew longer and warmer this spring, but she still has this pall of gloom that cannot be shaken. I am loath to leave her alone for long periods. Perhaps if Ethan were free. She always looked up to him."

Allen referred to his defiant older brother, who remained a prisoner of the British—a symbol of Vermont's spirit. Captured two years previously, he had not been released in the general armistice between the British and the Continentals, as he chose to consider himself a Vermonter first.

Warner's expression grew serious as he listened to Allen. "Have you news of Ethan?"

"No. But that's one of the reasons I was eager to go on this mission to Quebec. I will see if I can gain his release while I'm there. I think the council knows that too, though they can't make it part of my official charge. I haven't said anything about it to Lucy and won't, at least not until I know I can succeed in it."

"I wish you luck. It would be great to have him back; if it helps

Lucy, that would be even better. I sincerely hope she recovers soon. She always brought so much joy to our family gatherings."

"Thank you. Now, if you'll excuse me, I need to finish making arrangements for the trip."

"Come back to us soon, my dear cousin. May God assist you in accomplishing your mission." Warner watched him step away, then turned his attention back to the rangers' training.

———◄◊►———

Awe washed over Lucy Armistead. Vermont had never prepared her for this. As she, her brother, and the other three Vermont representatives approached Quebec City on horseback, the early morning sun cast a golden glow on the city's imposing stone walls. These fortifications encircled the city's crown, perched dramatically on cliffs overlooking the St. Lawrence River.

Lucy's eyes widened, and her mind was abuzz. "Marvelous," she mouthed silently. *I never dreamed of seeing a city like this. I must find a way to persuade Ira to let me explore this wonder. I'll curl up and die if he keeps me cooped up.*

Their journey took them through the bustling lower town. Lucy gripped her horse's reins tighter as they made their way slowly through the press of people in the street. The fetid odor of the sewers assaulted her senses. *I hope I can quickly become accustomed to this smell, for the sights are astonishing.* As they rode, the horses' rhythmic clip-clop echoed off the cobblestone streets, a novel sound for her against the backdrop of the vibrant city.

"Paved streets!" she exclaimed to Ira. "Have you ever seen anything like it? This must be the richest city in the world!" He hadn't seen her smile in a year, and a flicker of hope ignited within him. *Perhaps this city will be the cure she needs*, he thought.

"It's the biggest city I've seen," he replied. "And there are more people here than I've ever seen in one place." *Though this many redcoats make me a bit nervous.*

"Where are we staying, Ira?"

"Upper Town." He pointed toward the imposing stone buildings perched atop the hill. "That's where the governor and other military leaders are. They assured us quarters there for our stay."

Lucy's eyes followed her brother's outstretched arm, and she stared at the buildings along Upper Town's imposing wall. *What a marvelous view there must be from those buildings. They tower over the city like in a fairy tale.* Turning her head, she was captivated by the immediate streetscape. The buildings were a choreographed mix: two and three stories tall, their dormer windows jutting over the rooftops. Steep gabled roofs, dark slate tiles contrasting sharply with the cream and tan stone, some with smooth plastered facades. Towering wide chimneys rose above, and high firewalls marked the boundaries between them.

A sudden aroma was a welcome invasion to her senses. It was the unmistakable fragrance of freshly baked bread, yeasty and warm. Lucy's eyes landed on a charming bakery nestled amongst the shops. Customers bustled through the doorway, exiting with golden brown loaves of fresh bread tucked under their arms or carried in wicker baskets.

"Boulangerie Demange," Lucy deciphered the elegant lettering above the shop's entrance. "It smells delicious. Back home, I'm the one who kneads the dough and tends to the fire. All you have to do here is walk in and buy it!" The wonder in her voice was unmistakable. This was a world of convenience, a stark contrast to the life she knew, and it ignited a spark of curiosity within her.

The cobbled street snaked around a corner, revealing a sight that stole Lucy's breath. A staircase rose steeply toward Upper Town. Here, pedestrians hurried up and down the steps intent on reaching their destinations. On horseback, the traveling party needed to navigate the longer route, winding through the streets. The towers, ramparts, and parapets of Upper Town soon loomed over them. These same fortifications had withstood the American siege just three years before.

The street curved gently upward, and finally the Palais Gate pierced the imposing wall, marking an entrance to Upper Town. The thirty-foot stone walls were even more awe-inspiring at close range. As Lucy's group approached the gate, redcoats blocked their path, demanding they dismount and present their documents for approval before being allowed to enter. Ira retrieved a leather parcel from his coat, opened it, and offered the letters of invitation signed by the governor's aide-de-camp, Captain Theodore Brehm. A soldier brought the papers to his sergeant to review. Ira shifted his weight from one foot to the other as he waited, his eyes fixed on the gatehouse door, willing the soldier to reappear. When the soldier finally emerged, he trailed a sergeant, who held the letters.

"Good morning, sir," said the sergeant. "I'll need to have you escorted to your destination. My private here will guide you. Unfortunately, we have no spare horse for him. You will also need to walk, although you may take your horses with you. The lady, however,"—his eyes swept over Lucy—"may ride. I assume this is acceptable?"

"Absolutely, sergeant," Allen replied. "I'd appreciate an escort to help us navigate to our destination and avoid getting lost." *And not thinking we're spies*, he added to himself.

The private showed them the way through the gate. The slower pace allowed Lucy to take in Upper Town's architecture. It was just as marvelous as that of Lower Town, and numerous civilians were going about their business. However, more uniformed soldiers walked the streets.

"There it is," said the soldier, gesturing to a three-story house farther up the street, "the one with the madder red shutters." Once they stopped in front of the house, he added, "I'll take your horses to the stable over yonder," pointing farther up the street. "I'll ensure they're taken care of. Captain Brehm will be informed of your arrival."

"Thank you, Private," Allen replied.

Allen knocked at the door, and a servant answered. After explaining who they were, they were ushered inside. Several bedrooms, clearly prepared for their arrival, awaited them. "When you've settled in, I can fetch you some refreshments."

Left alone in her assigned room, Lucy found the modest-sized space well-appointed. A magnificent canopied four-poster bed dominated the space, accompanied by a writing table, chairs, a washbasin, and a chamber pot. A cedar chest tucked in the corner housed woolen blankets for the winter. Shelves lined a wall for folded clothes, and a row of pegs provided hanging space for others. The lower portion of the walls was painted a creamy white, capped by an ornate chair rail. Above, an earthy beige hue stretched across the expanse, adorned with portraits of stern-faced British officers.

The Vermonters met in the dining room, where the servant had laid out fresh bread, cheeses, jams, hard-boiled eggs, and small beer.

They sat and ate, discussing the sights of Quebec City. Their meal was interrupted by a messenger bearing a letter of invitation for dinner from Captain Brehm. The note promised an escort would arrive at quarter to six o'clock to take them to the dinner.

Chapter 3

Renaissance

Lucy stepped into the parlor wearing the finest dress she had brought: a floor-length checkered black-and-white petticoat, over which she had a pastel-green floral-print jacket with elbow-length sleeves that ended with ruffled lace. She hadn't worn this dress in more than a year. There hadn't been a need to. But tonight, she was partaking in her first dinner outside the confines of her Bennington family, unless you counted the night the baron had appeared. And that barely qualified anymore, as the baron had become ubiquitous in the Vermont Republic.

Almost a year after losing her husband, grief had cast a veil over everything, making each day feel distant and blurred. But here, amidst new sights and a place she had never imagined, a sliver of hope pierced her veil. Quebec City awaited, and with it, an official dinner on her very first evening here.

A carriage pulled up in front of the house promptly at a quarter to six o'clock. *A carriage! I've never ridden in a carriage before.* Excitement tinged with nervousness pulsed through her, and Lucy pressed her lips together to suppress a smile. The Vermonters stepped outside. *I feel like I've entered a different world.*

The carriage was pulled by a matched pair of chestnut-colored horses, their leather harnesses attached to the carriage just below the coachman's seat. The hunter green of the carriage's body matched the green canopy roof shading the seats within. The coachman opened the door and folded down a set of steps, allowing easy entry into the high cabin and revealing plush red velvet cushions, a promise of comfort and a striking contrast to the hard leather saddle of her journey. Closing the door behind them, the driver climbed to the raised seat in front, took the reins, gave them a quick shake, and clicked his tongue twice, at which sound the horses started forward. Polished brass lamps swayed on either side of the carriage as it rode along on large, black iron-rimmed wooden wheels rattling on the cobblestones.

A quarter-hour later, the carriage lurched to a halt before a stately three-story stone house. The coachman jumped down from his seat, opened the carriage door, and folded down the steps for their exit. Ira Allen emerged first, then turned to offer Lucy his hand as she stepped out. Waiting at the door, a uniformed servant bowed deeply, his powdered wig reflecting the last of the day's golden rays. He conducted them toward the parlor where Captain Theodore Brehm, his crimson jacket a vivid splash of color, dominated the entrance. His hand shot out in greeting, his military bearing belying the warmth in his amber eyes.

"Good evening, gentlemen," Brehm said, his voice a rich baritone. His gaze shifted to Lucy, and with a slight bow, he added, "And lady. I am Captain Theodore Brehm, at your service."

Ira introduced himself. "And this must be the lovely Mrs. Allen," interjected Brehm. He reached for her hand and brushed a kiss across her knuckles. Lucy blushed.

"Forgive me, Captain," Ira cut in. "This is my sister, Mrs. Armistead."

"Ahh. Forgive me. It is a pleasure to meet you, Mrs. Armistead."
Brehm turned toward the other Vermont representatives. "And which
of you is the lucky Mr. Armistead?"

Lucy's smile faded, and she cast her eyes downward as Ira stepped
forward. "Unfortunately, he has passed away."

"I am sorry to hear that." His clasp of Lucy's hand lingered a beat.

Ira introduced the others as Brehm greeted each in turn. "Will
Governor Haldimand be joining us this evening?" Ira asked.

"It is I who must apologize now," Brehm said, a hint of regret
in his voice. "The governor has been detained with some pressing
business. He entrusted me to entertain you for the evening. My staff
has prepared a delightful meal, but first, a diversion perhaps? I recently procured some exquisite claret, a welcome change from the usual
Madeira."

"Claret?" Ira leaned forward, a glint of interest in his eyes. Brehm
launched into a description of the wine, his voice animated.

"I've never had claret."

"Then you must try some. Here." Brehm picked up a decanter,
poured glasses, and handed them to Allen and his male companions.

Lucy tilted her head slightly and stared at Brehm. "Mrs. Armistead,
could I also interest you in some as well?"

"I would be delighted." She smiled. He repeated the process and
handed her the glass of wine. She took it, raised her glass, and said,
"Gentlemen, a toast to a successful resolution of your discussions,"
and took a sip.

"Hear, hear," cheered Brehm. *She is a most intriguing woman*, he
thought. "How were your travels?" he asked the assembled.

"It was a pleasant enough journey," Ira replied. "The weather cooperated. There were no sudden rainstorms that are so prevalent this time of year. I must say, the city presented an impressive sight as we approached."

"And even more impressive sights when we entered," Lucy said. "There were so many charming shops I would love to explore. Perhaps Mrs. Brehm would be so kind as to show me around the city."

"Alas, there is no Mrs. Brehm."

Something stirred in Lucy's chest, an ember of curiosity long dormant. "How unfortunate. I shall, I'm sure, find an alternative. The little we saw on our way has me fascinated with the city."

"I'll see what can be arranged, Mrs. Armistead." Reluctantly turning his gaze away from Lucy, he continued, "Shall we retire to the dining room for the first course? And we can discuss the plans for tomorrow."

He turned back to Lucy. "May I escort you, Mrs. Armistead?" Lucy nodded as Brehm hooked his arm in hers and they strode to the dining room.

———◦———

The next day dawned crisp, a familiar feeling for Lucy, who had spent her lifetime in the green mountains of Vermont. After breakfast, a messenger arrived with a letter addressed to Mrs. Armistead. Lucy opened it with anticipation.

She scanned the letter, then read aloud. "Mrs. Armistead, I have procured a guide for your visit to Quebec City, Mrs. Adelaide Johnson, the wife of a close friend. She stated she would be delighted to escort you on your travels around the city. Expect her arrival at nine o'clock. Your servant, Capt. Brehm." Lucy could not hide her pleasure this time as a broad smile enveloped her face. Ira Allen smiled in return.

"I'd better get ready," Lucy said as she rose. "Gentlemen," she curt-sied, still smiling. "I shall see you this evening."

Ira stared after her, his smile lingering as well. *It's good to see her happy*, he thought. Turning to the others in the room, he said, "Well, we ought to get this started. Hopefully, this proves to be a fruitful day for Vermont."

The men left the house and walked a quarter-hour to the meeting location at the governor general's compound. The steady drum of their leather shoes against the stone street served as background noise to Ira's thoughts. *My duty is to Vermont. But I must find a way to free Ethan. He's been held for so long.* He only snapped back to reality as they were confronted by two uniformed soldiers. Ira fumbled for their letter of invitation in his coat pocket, then presented it to the stony-faced guards protecting the entrance.

Inside, the home had a strong French influence, with parquet hard-wood floors leading to a large fireplace with an ornately carved mantel. The walls were covered with paintings of uniformed soldiers, country hunting scenes, and various scenes of the Quebec region, both city and countryside. After a while, they were greeted by a steely Captain Brehm, his face a mask of military formality. He informed them that Governor Haldimand was waiting for them and led them to the meeting room.

—◆—

Ira paced Lucy's room while waiting for dinner to be served. "Damn him. He refused to budge from his position. It's infuriating."

"What position?" Lucy asked, closing the book she had borrowed from the home's library.

"It was all pleasant enough," Ira huffed. "They're the epitome of decorum. But bring up a simple request to stop the Yorkers from initiating attacks on our people, and we're met with a stone wall. Haldimand wouldn't even consider the request unless we first agreed that our republic renounce independence and rejoin the British Empire. That was his starting point, and he did not diverge from it."

"I hope you weren't shouting at him like a madman," Lucy said, shaking her head.

Ira stopped and looked at Lucy. "I did not. I kept my composure. We need to figure out how to move him off that position and get him to negotiate. We're meeting again the day after tomorrow."

"Was Captain Brehm there?" Lucy asked, feigning nonchalance.

Ira furrowed his brows. "Why?"

"Just that he seemed to be a nice soul, maybe even sympathetic to our cause."

"Likely because you were there and the governor was not."

"Then maybe we can use the time between now and your next meeting to find a wedge to break the governor's position," Lucy said.

"And what could that be?"

"I don't know," Lucy said. "What's in it for him? Or Britain? What do we have that he cannot get elsewhere?"

"Our land," Ira answered grimly.

"No. There must be something else. Mrs. Johnson mentioned today that there is considerable relief now that the war has ended. They want peace. How can we use that?"

"Mrs. Johnson said that? Did she have anything else to say?" Ira said, his interest piqued.

"Well, not about that. But she's taking me out again tomorrow."

Ira grinned. "Captain Johnson was at the negotiations as well. I wonder if he confides in his wife. See what else she might let slip."

A veil of heavy clouds shrouded the city, and a steady rain washed away the grime that had clung to the cobblestones and brick facades. The air held the earthy scent of summer rain, a welcome reprieve from the city's usual stench. Lucy stood beneath the portico, listening to the comforting rhythm of the rain on its roof. Rounding a corner at the end of the row of homes, a familiar burgundy carriage emerged from the mist. Lucy waved as the horse and carriage drew closer.

"Good morning, Mrs. Johnson," Lucy greeted Adelaide as the driver let down the steps for her.

Adelaide adjusted the white kerchief covering her caramel-colored hair. "Good morning, Mrs. Armistead. Though I am sorry for this weather," she said, her brown eyes warm despite her apology.

"Oh, don't be. It reminds me of a summer morning in Vermont, minus our beautiful trees, of course." Lucy laughed, a moment of genuine joy that surprised even her. "What do you have planned for today?"

"Have you had any breakfast? I thought we could start with a visit to a delightful little bakery I frequent, Boulangerie Demange."

Lucy's eyes widened. "I noticed it the day we arrived!"

"You must try their raspberry tarts; they are simply divine. And their bread is heavenly. I like it so much better than the white bread our kitchen bakes. My mouth waters just thinking about it."

The carriage jostled as they navigated the streets, already teeming with people despite the gloomy weather. The city pulsed with a vibrant energy that was both foreign and oddly invigorating to Lucy. As they arrived at the bakery, the rainfall turned into a downpour. Not waiting for the driver, Adelaide pushed down the steps of the carriage and scurried down with Lucy in close pursuit. They entered the store laughing, brushing the rain from their dresses. Lucy adjusted her hat, whose turned-up edges had collected a pool of water that spilled onto her, soaking her. Adelaide looked her over and burst out laughing again.

"We're going to have to do something about that dress," Adelaide said. "But first, I promised you the best tarts in Quebec."

They lingered a while in the bakery, hoping the rain would slow. In addition to the tarts Adelaide purchased as a gift for her, Lucy bought two of the recommended French breads. Once the rain slowed to a drizzle, they exited the store to their waiting carriage.

"Where to next?" Lucy asked, her voice bright with anticipation.

"I have the perfect place: Madame Roux's. I must find a new dress. And maybe we can find you something dryer." Adelaide giggled.

"That's all right. This will dry out."

"But you'll need something for the party the governor is hosting. My husband said you all are invited."

"Party? I'm not aware of any party. Are you sure?"

"Oh yes. In fact, he specifically mentioned your brother." She leaned close and added in a whisper, "Captain Brehm will be there."

Lucy ignored her comment. "I already have a good dress with me. I can wear that."

"Oh, I'm sure something will catch your eye at Madame Roux's," Adelaide said with a roguish grin.

The carriage slowed as more people filled the street now that the rain had stopped. Sunlight from breaks in the clouds streamed through the carriage windows, revealing a brilliant sapphire sky. Lucy was engrossed by the sights around her, swiveling her head so as not to miss anything. Madame Roux's was housed in a tan stone building with deep-red shutters and a matching roof. Exiting the carriage, Lucy stopped to admire the dressmaker's dummy in the window, which was fitted with an ivory floral print cotton dress, open in the front revealing a crimson petticoat beneath.

"It's not going to try itself on," Adelaide said. "Come on in. Let's see if it fits you."

They were greeted by Madame Roux, a middle-aged woman who retained the beauty of her youth, her once ginger hair now a faded rosy blonde. Adelaide was obviously known to her and took charge of the conversation and introductions. Madame Roux looked Lucy over. "Perhaps with a few minor alterations, yes, I think it will fit." She stepped over to the mannequin and lifted the dress over and off. "Come with me, Mrs. Armistead. Let's see what I can do to help you with this."

Lucy returned, practically dancing into the room, exuberant. The floral print dress pinned by Madame Roux swayed as she moved. She looked herself over in the mirror while Adelaide admired it.

"It's perfect," Adelaide gushed.

"I don't know. I'm not sure my brother would approve."

"Oh, fiddlesticks. You simply must buy it."

Just then, Captain Brehm stepped into the shop. "I thought that was your carriage and driver," he exclaimed when he saw Lucy. "How fortunate to run into you!"

Lucy glanced suspiciously at Adelaide, who only shrugged. "Captain Brehm, it's nice to see you again," Lucy greeted him, "though it's certainly a surprise. I would have thought you had more pressing business."

"I do, or at least did, in this part of the city. I've already taken care of that. And what could be more pressing than to say hello? What a beautiful dress, especially on you, Mrs. Armistead."

"Do you really think so?" She glanced again in the mirror.

"I told her it would be perfect for the party," Adelaide said.

"And I told Mrs. Johnson I had not heard anything about a party," Lucy said.

Captain Brehm laughed. "The invitation will be delivered today. The governor requested some last-minute changes." He studied the dress for a moment, as if gathering courage. "That dress would be perfect for the party," he said, then added more quietly, "It looks lovely on you."

"I can have this altered for you tomorrow," Madame Roux said, who had been listening to the conversation. "You can get changed, and I'll start working on it."

Lucy smiled and walked back to get changed. Captain Brehm stepped over to speak privately with Madame Roux, telling her to deliver the completed dress to the Vermonters' quarters and the bill to him.

Golden rays sliced through gaps in the clouds as the trio left the shop and walked to the Johnson carriage, which the driver had moved a few stores away to wait. Lucy stopped at a stationer's shop to get a better look at a wooden chess set in the window.

"Do you play, Mrs. Armistead?" Captain Brehm sidled beside her.

Her smile of remembrance faded and she cast her eyes to the pavement. "I used to play with my brother. I haven't in a while."

"With Mr. Allen?"

"Not that brother. My eldest brother, Ethan. He taught me after our father's death to distract me."

"Oh, I'm so sorry. Has he passed too?"

"No." Lucy turned away from Captain Brehm, pulling a handkerchief from her pocket to dab at her eyes.

"What is it, Mrs. Armistead? What have I done to upset you?"

"I've been having such a good time that I almost let myself forget." She turned to him. "You're holding him prisoner."

He stepped back at the accusatory tone. "Me?"

"Well, not you, specifically. The British. For almost three years now. He wasn't released with the general amnesty granted when the Americans surrendered. The last we heard of him, he was imprisoned in New York City. But now we don't even know if he's alive." The tears she had been holding back now gushed.

Adelaide moved closer and gave her a hug, at the same time looking at Captain Brehm and mouthing, "Do something."

Bewildered, he shrugged. "Mrs. Armistead, I can make inquiries, but please understand that this is outside my authority."

"Will you? Oh, thank you!" Lucy managed a modest smile.

Captain Brehm escorted the ladies the rest of the way to their carriage, waited for them to get in, and watched them depart. On the way to retrieve his horse, he stepped inside the stationer's shop.

———— ◆ ————

The governor was playing his own game. Haldimand had decided to concede a point—the New York militia would hold fire. There would be no attacks on Vermonters or the land claimed by Vermont east of Lake Champlain. But the governor's voice had turned steely as he warned the Vermont delegation that any aggression from the republic would unleash retaliation. New Yorkers would defend themselves and their lands and homes.

After the meeting, Captain Brehm saw his opening and spoke privately with the governor. "Ethan Allen's imprisonment, sir," he ventured. "Perhaps releasing him as a gesture of goodwill could pave the way for productive talks?" The governor's narrowed eyes revealed his intrigue with the idea.

Captain Brehm pulsed with nervous energy as he worked at his desk. The negotiations with the Vermonters had concluded for the day. He turned over Governor Haldimand's words in his mind: Prepare for Vermont. He was to travel and stay in Vermont as the governor's representative for continued negotiations with the Vermont Council. Elation clashed with a pang of doubt. *What if the negotiations fail? More time with Lucy, though, is a thrilling prospect.* He glanced at the small carved wooden box at the corner of his desk—a chess set, a gift for her. Anxiety crept over his joy. *Will the gift spark cherished memories or only the sting of loss, a well of tears I desperately want to spare her? Maybe waiting is wiser.*

Captain Brehm was writing Haldimand's letter to General Sir Henry Clinton in New York City, ordering the cessation of militia activity against Vermont and Ethan Allen's return to Bennington. With luck, Ethan would be there when the Vermont representatives, Lucy, and he arrived. *All this will be worth it to see her light up with joy when she reunites with her brother*, he thought.

Next up, though, was the governor's party, which was a few days away. The Vermonters had accepted their invitations, and he fidgeted in anticipation, smiling as he imagined Lucy in her new dress. *I haven't danced in so long; I hope I don't make a fool of myself.* He laughed out loud. *It'll still be worth it just to spend time with Lucy.*

Chapter 4

Bennington

"This is some beautiful countryside," Brehm remarked, standing on the deck watching the countryside slide by. "I haven't been this far south from Quebec." They were sailing south on the Connecticut River in a two-masted pink, a flat-bottomed ship ideal for sailing in the shallower river, and were nearing their port destination of Brattleboro. From there, they would travel west overland to Bennington.

"Wait until you see the Green Mountains," Ira Allen said. "They're teeming with beech, birch, and sugar maple." He smacked his lips at the thought of the sugar maples. "Have you ever tasted our syrup from the maple tree?"

"I encountered it upon my arrival in Quebec, but I've never had the opportunity to have any. How do you make it?"

"I daresay you must try it while here," Ira exclaimed. "I have a jug at home collected this past spring."

Lucy interjected. "We hammer a tap into trees in late winter before the sap starts to run and hang buckets to collect it. Then we boil it down in kettles to thicken it and store it in jugs for the year. You can use it to sweeten meals. I even use it when baking bread."

"It's great to use straight from the jug on flapjacks," Ira added.

"And I remember Mother scolding you for how much you used!"

The siblings shared easy smiles.

Ira cherished these moments of the old Lucy returning. The trip to Quebec had sparked a change. *I suspect Captain Brehm has played a part in that*, he thought. *I've noticed the captain's gaze on Lucy more than once, and they hadn't missed a dance at the governor's ball. But I can't let this cloud my judgment or affect our negotiations. Captain Brehm still represents everything we oppose. We cannot lose this fight.*

"And the sugar maples put on a wondrous display come autumn," Lucy was saying, "turning the mountains into a fiery sunset with shades of orange, reds, and yellows."

"I look forward to seeing that," Brehm said.

"Hopefully, your discussions with the Vermont Council conclude long before then," Ira said.

"How long to reach Bennington once we dock?" Brehm asked.

"Four or five days should do it," Ira replied.

Captain Brehm made some mental calculations. "That may work out then," he said under his breath.

"What may work out?" Lucy asked.

Brehm paused. While relieved to share the news about her brother's potential release, he considered his words. "I was intending it to be a surprise. I still hope it coincides with the start of talks."

"What?" Lucy pressed, while Ira cocked his head.

"Governor Haldimand wrote General Clinton in New York ordering that your brother be released and sent back home as a gesture of goodwill."

Lucy inhaled sharply and placed her hand over her heart. "You said it was beyond your control—that there wasn't anything you could do about it! But you did it! Oh, Captain Brehm, you've made me so happy."

Ira's smile faded. "Lucy, you asked Captain Brehm to get Ethan released?"

"She didn't ask me," Brehm responded. "Mrs. Armistead let slip that he was still being held our prisoner. Frankly, Mr. Allen, my feeling is he was captured as a Continental, and he should have been released in the general armistice. I'm happy to have played a small part in it." His expression darkened with unease. "I hope he's there when we get there. There was not enough time to receive word back from General Clinton before our departure."

Has Lucy accomplished what I could not? Ira thought. *All throughout our negotiations he never hinted that he knew about Ethan. I felt he was clever, but I must be doubly attentive now.*

———◦———

Word reached the party one evening from a traveler who had left Bennington that morning: Their brother, Ethan, had returned home. Lucy, unable to contain her anticipation, started the camp fire and had the group's breakfast ready before anyone else was up. In truth, she hadn't gotten much sleep that night in her excitement about reaching Bennington.

As the first rays of dawn reached the Green Mountains, they mounted their horses and rode west. By late afternoon, Bennington's familiar silhouette greeted them. Lucy raced out ahead of her traveling companions, kicking up dust as she spurred her steed into a gallop. Ira, following her lead, urged his horse after her. The others trotted into town, and Captain Brehm was directed to the Dewey Inn, which would be his quarters for the duration of his stay.

The windows and door to the inn's tavern were open, allowing fresh air and the breeze inside and the aroma of roasting meat and the murmur of conversation out. Captain Brehm entered and stopped in the doorway until his eyes adjusted to the dimmer light. His imposing stature, the fact that he was blocking light from the door, and, most notably, his crimson uniform caught the eyes of the patrons inside. The buzz of conversation stopped abruptly.

General Seth Warner's booming voice broke the silence. "Captain Theodore Brehm, I presume."

Captain Brehm scrutinized the tall man, around his age, wearing the dark green ranger regimental and a general's insignia. "It's a pleasure to meet you, General Warner." He strode forward, smiling and extending his hand in greeting.

Warner glanced over Brehm's shoulder toward the tavern's door and asked, "Did not Mr. Allen and Mrs. Armistead accompany you here?"

"Yes, indeed. They rode ahead as we approached, I assume, to see their brother."

"Ah, yes. So word already reached you about his release? We appreciate your role in securing Colonel Allen's freedom, Captain."

"I played but a small part." Brehm bowed slightly. "It was Governor Haldimand who secured his release."

"The Vermont Council has been in session these past few days, and your arrival is most timely. Have you eaten yet?"

"No. And the aroma as I approached has my mouth watering."

"Excellent. Sit with me and refresh yourself. There is much to discuss."

Captain Brehm sat on the worn wooden bench as the weight of the Vermont negotiations settled on his shoulders.

With General Warner preoccupied in Bennington for negotiations, Baron von Steuben assumed direct command of the Green Mountain Rangers. The frequent Yorker raids into Vermont territory had ceased. Still, the baron remained vigilant, positioning his men northwest of Bennington along the Little White Creek. This creek, a disputed boundary between Vermont and New York, had been the epicenter of most territorial conflicts.

Von Steuben made his temporary headquarters on a hilltop, which gave him a commanding view of the surroundings. Bennington was visible through his spyglass three miles to his southeast. Every so often, travelers could be seen taking the road into the town. Locals usually were on foot, while those more distant were on horseback, wagon, and the occasional coach. Based on the baron's acquired knowledge of Bennington and the trade conducted there, these were likely to be Yorkers. Despite the past militia skirmishes, each side needed the other as a trading partner. Peace would benefit all, and the baron hoped the negotiations would be successful.

The baron rode north in the mornings, along with his ever-present companion, du Ponceau, to inspect his troops and ensure the officers were on guard for surprises. But this morning, du Ponceau seemed preoccupied.

The baron paused on a hilltop taking in the commanding view. He enjoyed these excursions through the Green Mountains, which he had started to think of as home. He sat upon his horse, gazing at the mist rising from the forests after a brief rain shower. *I could live here when this is over,* he thought. *A farm, cows, sheep, maybe enough maple trees to capture that syrup I've grown to love. And while I would never admit as much to General Warner, I'm satisfied with how well the rangers are performing.*

"Friedrich, there's been something on my mind," du Ponceau said, interrupting the baron's thoughts. The baron gave him a quizzical look. "This place is stifling me. I believe I know everyone in Bennington by name."

"And? What would you have us do?" von Steuben said, with a hint of irritation. "I have a job to do, and a nation to defend. They've entrusted me with securing Bennington while the Englishman is here."

"I didn't say I wanted an immediate change," du Ponceau shot back, his face scrunched into a scowl. "If they're successful, perhaps there'll be an opportunity for something more. Something different. Maybe visit Quebec City or Philadelphia." He caught sight of the baron's frown. "I was hoping for more," his voice trailed off.

Von Steuben let out a gruff huff. "Nothing more to see here. Let's head back to camp."

They rode in silence through another shower before they had completed their journey. The scent of earth and loam filled their nostrils.

———•◦•———

Captain Brehm's presence in Bennington and his negotiations with the Vermont Council were not a well-kept secret. Instead, they were the main topic of conversation at the Dewey Tavern. Not that anyone with direct knowledge of the discussions was talking about them, but the captain's mere presence, along with that of General Seth Warner and the council representatives, was enough to get eager tongues wagging, especially in a small town.

The Dewey Tavern was the only inn in town. Anyone having business in the area or just passing through ended up there. Captain Brehm found himself not at a loss for people who wanted to meet and speak with him. This evening, weary from a long week of discussions, he wanted only to eat his supper and review the day's discussions. Once again, he had an uninvited visitor at his table asking pointed questions about when negotiations would conclude.

"Excuse me, Mr. Smith, is it?" Brehm asked. His tablemate nodded. "Well, Mr. Smith, I'll be forthright with you since you've asked about negotiations between Vermont and the British Empire, just as you attempted to a few days ago. Not that you were in any way respectful in your clumsy attempt at conversation." Brehm's voice had risen, and a few of the locals stopped their discussions to listen. "What if I told you I'm here on personal business? Just like you claim. Here to make arrangements for the wheat harvest, is it? Mr. Smith, what farmers have you met with in the last few days? I recall you sitting in the tavern here yesterday, right over there." He pointed to a table in the corner of the room. "I think it best you stick with your business and not anyone else's. Good evening, sir." Mr. Smith, his mouth agape, slunk out of the tavern, eyes of a curious tavern folk on him. Brehm hunched over his now-cold chicken stew. *At least the applejack whiskey still has its kick*, he thought as he downed a swig.

A few minutes later, Brehm saw the shadow of another patron sit down on his bench. He breathed a heavy sigh and turned to confront the intruder. "Mr. Allen, I didn't expect you."

"I saw your heated exchange with that gentleman," Ethan Allen said. Ethan looked older than his forty years, and his thinning hair was streaked with gray, though his long thin face had an easy smile. He wore brown breeches with a green waistcoat that was just a tad loose on him. Brehm surmised he had lost weight during his imprisonment. "I'd wager a guinea to a penny he was a Yorker seeking information." His nostrils flared in disgust.

"We've heard rumors about that. Still, they'll get no information from me."

"But there will be others. I don't like it. I don't think you should lodge here."

Brehm raised his eyebrows. "Where else would I stay?"

"With me. I have room. My home is just across the way. And you'd be away from prying eyes—and ears."

And I'd probably get to see Lucy more if I accepted, Brehm thought. "An intriguing offer, Mr. Allen. Though I would have thought you would not want a British officer in your home."

"In the first place, you were responsible for getting me released." Brehm started to object, but Allen continued. "No, no, you were. And I have not properly thanked you for that kindness." He leaned close to Brehm and added, "And if we are to have peace, we must live in peace. What better way than to put that on display?"

"Well, Mr. Allen," Brehm said, thrusting out his arm for a handshake, "I'd like that very much."

Beneath bales of wool, Samuel Fairbanks could barely breathe, confined in the back of the wagon bumping down a rocky path that served as a road. His hands were bound behind him, and a gag muffled his protests. He contemplated how it had come to this. Fairbanks had fought with the New York militia against the British in a few battles, but that was before Vermont declared independence. At that point, he left the militia to volunteer with the Green Mountain Rangers, where he had been appointed lieutenant colonel. Fairbanks had recently received word that the New York militia had conscripted him as a private, ordering him to report to Albany. He'd ignored the order. *I'm a Vermonter. They have no power over me, and I have no interest in fighting for the crown, especially after the Continentals' surrender. But the Yorkers obviously disagreed. Kidnapped from my own home! Dragged out like a common criminal, my wife screaming in terror. It's been hours since they gave me anything to eat. What are their intentions?*

The wagon lurched to a halt. The bales were heaved off, and Fairbanks squinted in the sudden glare of the sun. Before he could fully adjust to the light, his two burly captors roughly hauled him from the wagon bed, his feet scraping the ground. They hustled him into a brick building, where he caught a fleeting glimpse of a wooden sign inscribed with a single word above the doorway: JAIL.

Once inside, they dragged him before the jailer sitting behind a desk. A sturdy man, with a full black beard with flecks of gray, his close-set eyes were barely open. The two men held Fairbanks between them while the jailor looked him over. "Is this him?" the jailer drawled. At their nod, he chuckled. "Lock him in that cell." He gestured toward a cramped, metal-barred enclosure. "You're under arrest for desertion from the New York militia," and added with a sneer, "Private."

The men shoved him toward the cell, roughly yanking off his restraints and tossing him inside before slamming the metal door shut with a resounding clang. Fairbanks scrambled to his feet, gripping the cold bars that confined him. "I am Lieutenant Colonel Samuel Fairbanks of the Vermont Republic! You have no authority over me!"

"There is no Vermont Republic," the jailer scoffed. "You're a citizen of New York and subject to our laws. You failed to appear for your militia duty and will face the consequences."

"You won't get away with this!" Fairbanks roared.

"We already have," the jailer retorted. "No one's coming to save you." He jingled the cell keys in his pocket before turning to his companions. "Let's go get a drink." The men filed out, leaving Fairbanks alone with his anger.

Chapter 5

Retribution and Reckoning

News of Fairbanks's kidnapping spread quickly through the Green Mountains even before the wagon carrying him away arrived in Albany. Word of his likely destination arrived through travelers who passed a wagon and riders galloping west on the Albany Road. His kinfolk and fellow rangers organized an impromptu rescue mission. Eight men shed their uniforms and rode in civilian garb toward Albany to seek information on Fairbanks's whereabouts. Once there, they agreed to split up in pairs and head to various taverns and local shops, anywhere loose tongues might wag. They would meet again in an hour's time to exchange information. As darkness fell, two rangers, seeking whispers among the inebriated patrons, ventured into the Black Horse Inn's tavern, close to the only jail in town. The dimly lit establishment buzzed with activity. Spotting an empty table near the back wall, they made their way to it and ordered ales. Absorbing their surroundings, they listened intently to the din of conversations punctuated by the clinking of mugs and bursts of laughter.

Suddenly, a booming voice cut through the din. "The look on his face! 'You won't get away with this!'" The speaker guffawed as he lifted his tankard.

The rangers exchanged glances.

"He's not going anywhere locked away in that jail cell. We'll just let him stew in there for a while." The same voice laughed again. "I dare those Green Mountain fools to show their faces here. They'd flee at the first sight of our boys peppering them with lead." He nodded at his companions. "You boys wrapped him up tighter than those bales of wool!" He swallowed the last of his ale and called for another.

The rangers finished their ales and each tossed a shilling on the table before slipping out and memorizing the boastful men's faces as they passed.

Outside, a plan hatched. One ranger stayed hidden, keeping watch on the inn's entrance. The other located their companions at their agreed upon meeting point. Returning within the hour to the lookout spot around the corner from the Black Horse Inn, they shared news of what they'd learned. Nathaniel Reed and his nephew Jacob Thomas volunteered to reconnoiter around the jail, breaking Fairbanks out and spirit him away if possible. They slipped off toward the jail.

The remaining men lay in wait for the drunken kidnappers. One man retrieved a wagon—its origin left unspoken—and concealed it a short distance away.

No lantern lit the jail's interior. Reed and Thomas kept watch from around the corner. The lateness of the hour meant there were no passersby. Thomas kept watch out front; Reed circled around the building. He noted a rear door along a darkened alleyway. Peering closer, the hinges seemed rusty, the nails loose. He kicked the door. The thump echoed through the alleyway. *Better to get this done quickly*, he thought. *Thump*. The door shifted but did not break free. One last kick and the doorway was clear. He listened.

"Who's there?" came a voice from within.

Reed held his breath. *Was there a watchman within?* He placed his hand on his flintlock pistol.

"Is anybody there? Help me get out of here."

Reed exhaled. "Colonel Fairbanks?"

"Oh, thank the Lord. Get me out of this cell."

Reed went through the darkened corridor, emerging into a small room with a cell in the corner. He could barely make out a form in the meager moonlight streaming in the single window. "Colonel?"

"Yes. They've locked me in here. There's a lantern on the desk over there. See if you can light it and find the keys."

Reed felt his way toward the desk. "We need to move swiftly before that racket I made attracts any unwanted attention." He made quick work of getting a lantern candle lit with a small striker and flint he pulled from his pocket, illuminating the room. Holding the lantern, he examined the cell. There was no way he was going to be able to burst this open; he needed the key. Rummaging through the desk turned up nothing.

Suddenly, Reed became aware of footsteps behind him. "Watch out!" shouted Fairbanks. Reed readied to throw a punch.

"Whoa!" Thomas stepped back. "There are townsfolk approaching. We can't stay."

"You can't leave me in here," Fairbanks insisted.

"We need another plan. We'll be back," Thomas whispered to Fairbanks. "Come on, Uncle Nathaniel. Before it's too late." As they exited through the backdoor, several people entered the front. The lantern still burned, illuminating the open exit.

Reed and Thomas stole their way back to the men who had been waiting for the drunken kidnappers. The rangers were waiting, having captured the men who, to their misfortune, had stumbled out of the tavern into the deserted road. As the two men shambled off, the rangers had emerged from the shadows, rendering them unconscious with swift blows. They then half-carried and half-dragged the captives to the waiting wagon.

Just after Reed and Thomas arrived, a group of townsfolk rounded the corner.

"There!" came the shouts. "They're the ones!" "Get them!"

The rangers clambered on their horses, and the wagon whisked their captives northward toward the Green Mountains as the Yorkers chased after them.

◆◈◆

News reached John Jay, New York's governor, not of Fairbanks's kidnapping and imprisonment but of the abduction of their own men. Fury consumed him. His wide set eyes darted among the gathered. The nostrils of his broad nose flared. Lieutenant Caleb Griffith of the New York militia, an aide to the new governor, stood in his office, still in his uniform, the color of clotted cream, with cardinal facings, bearing the brunt of Jay's diatribe. In his forties, a decade older and a head shorter than the pacing governor, Griffith clenched his teeth. His deep brown eyes followed the shouting Jay about the room.

"I want them back," Jay roared, locks of his sandy bronze hair escaping his black queue ribbon. "Do those Vermonters think they can waltz into Albany and kidnap our citizens without consequences? The militia is here to protect us. Even the British military recognized this in the final agreement." Jay referenced the surrender agreement; though it disbanded and disarmed Continental soldiers, it allowed local provincial militias to remain armed to protect against Indian attack. "This is an attack by Vermont. I will not sit idly by while our people are molested. And I most certainly will not wait for approval from General Sir Henry Clinton in New York City. I want a regiment ready to march into Bennington and retrieve our people—by force if necessary. If we interrupt the peace negotiations with that council of theirs, then so much the better. They're taking away New York land without even involving us!"

"Do you think that wise, sir?" Lieutenant Griffith ventured.

"Wise?" Jay stopped pacing long enough to glare at Griffith, nostrils flaring. "What would you have us do? Capitulate our sovereignty to those motley scoundrels?" He sat at his desk, pulled a sheaf of paper, dipped his quill in the inkwell, and began to write orders for the militia. When done, he handed them to Griffith. "Here. Make sure these are executed. I want you with the force when it leaves tomorrow. Your skills as a physician may be needed."

"Yes, sir. I'll ensure they're ready, sir." Griffith left the office, closing the door behind him.

<hr/>

The military expedition started just after dawn the next day. Lieutenant Caleb Griffith's leather case of medications, herbs, and surgical tools was securely strapped to the horse he was riding alongside Colonel Allen Billingsley, the overall commander of the regiment. The militia comprised seven companies, each with about forty men led by a captain.

The first part of the journey was undemanding. They marched north, ferrying across the Hudson River just north of Albany. It took several crossings to ferry the entire regiment, delaying their advance an hour before resuming the journey east on the Albany Road. Traveling through undisputed New York territory, their demeanor was almost jovial. By all appearances, this was no more than a militia exercise, albeit larger than usual. But every step they took led them closer to Vermont—and danger.

Trees grew thick to the road's edge, providing shade for the men from the summer's heat. A midday respite allowed the men to eat from the provisions they had brought with them. Hitting the road once again, they marched east before turning on the Old Hoosick Road, which would lead northeast toward Bennington.

"Tighten up that column!" came a shout from one company commander. "You're sloppy! Keep those formations tight!"

Colonel Billingsley turned and saw his regiment stretching behind him. The crooked line of men was ill-suited for a military mission. Billingsley turned to Griffith. "Ride back to each captain. Inform them that my expectations are that they keep their men in proper order."

Griffith gave a curt nod. "Yes, sir."

"And Lieutenant, ensure they understand that if I should see such disorganization again, there will be the devil to pay."

As the sun grew lower in the cloudless sky, Colonel Billingsley ordered camp to be set up for the night in a meadow through which a creek flowed. Men supplemented their carried rations with rabbit and deer hunted from the forest around them.

The following day started off steamier than usual, with the heat building throughout the morning. Once again, Billingsley and Griffith rode at the vanguard of the column.

Griffith gazed at the sun, still low in the cloudless sky. Removing his hat, he wiped his forehead with a handkerchief. "This heat is stifling and will likely only get worse. May I suggest that the men be allowed to remove their regimental coats and carry them?"

Billingsley considered him for a moment. "We still have a considerable distance." He nodded. "Give the order."

The terrain changed from forested to hilly meadow, the blazing sun oppressive. Though the heat left the men's linen shirts soaked with sweat, removing their wool coats had provided welcome relief.

Camp was established that evening on the New York side of Little White Creek. Some of the younger men, who hadn't been in any battles during the recently concluded rebellion, exchanged boasts about the anticipated fight ahead. Others, who knew the true cost of conflict, remained silent, their thoughts to themselves.

The following day, they would cross the creek into the disputed territory of Vermont. And then on to Bennington to free their kidnapped brethren.

—◦—

Lucy stood at the wooden worktable in the unattached brick building kitchen of Ira Allen's home. She kneaded the dough for that day's bread using a new recipe Adelaide had given her. She gazed out the large window at Bennington's familiar landscape. Beyond the cultivated farmland, low-lying hills shaded in deep green trees rolled into steeper mountains, their peaks embraced by clouds. Earlier, while she was preparing the ingredients for the bread, she saw Captain Brehm taking the path hugging the edge of the orchard on his way to that day's negotiations.

Am I disrespecting Elias's memory by feeling this way? she wondered as her hands instinctively stretched, folded, and pressed the dough. *Elias, my beloved, I never thought I could feel anything again after you. But Quebec changed something in me. Captain Brehm changed something in me. Seeing Theodore makes me happy,* she admitted to herself. *But what does that say about me? Am I betraying Elias by finding joy with someone else? But don't I deserve to be happy? Don't I deserve a second chance?*

She closed her eyes, picturing Elias's face. The memory was bittersweet, and her eyes teared up. *Elias, I will always love you. But does that mean I must remain in this ghost walk forever? There are more things in heaven and earth—and I see that now.*

Ethan had noticed the change in her. And she surmised he had spoken about it to Ira. *Is that why Ethan had invited Captain Brehm to stay with him? He knows I'll get to see Theodore more that way. Perhaps it is his way of giving his approval.* She was struck by a sudden thought: *Are they using me to try to take advantage in negotiations with Captain Brehm? Am I a pawn in this game of chess?* The thought made her stomach churn. *But what of my dear Vermont? Can I help maintain her independence?*

She made a silent promise to herself. *I will navigate these conflicting emotions. I will honor Elias's memory, but I will also allow myself to explore this new path with Theodore. For the first time in a long time, I feel I have a future worth looking forward to.*

⊷◉⊶

Baron von Steuben sat at his desk in his headquarters' tent, eating breakfast. Outside, two privates stood guard, one at each front corner of the tent. The sun was clouded over, but no rain threatened. It hadn't rained in a few weeks, and the ground was hard and dry. After finishing breakfast, the baron emerged from his tent with an early-season apple, observing the morning bustle of his command post. From this hilltop, the baron had an almost complete view of the surrounding area—roads leading into and out of Bennington, part of the town itself, and approaches from New York. As he bit into his apple, a dust cloud rose among the trees to the north. Watching it move, he reached for his spyglass in his breast pocket, aiming it at the road that emerged from the woods. A rider! Speeding this way and in civilian garb. No sign of any others. The baron barked an order to intercept the man, and several horsemen galloped after him.

The rider brought news—an officer kidnapped and retaliation by his community. The baron gathered the unfolding details, frowning as he heard the tale spun. *This will lead to trouble*, he thought. "You're with me," von Steuben relayed to the messenger through du Ponceau. "We're going to Bennington now. I need to confer with General Warner."

In less than an hour, the three men trotted into town, the familiar dark shadow of Azor running beside his master's horse. Warner left the Vermont Council discussions when the baron arrived and met with them in an antechamber. The messenger repeated the news to Warner, and Warner asked clarifying questions.

Once they dismissed the messenger to wait for further instructions, the military men spoke openly. "The Yorkers won't stand for this," von Steuben warned. "They've refrained from open attacks since the British orders, but there'll be no hesitation now."

Warner stroked his chin. "I'm sure they'll claim we attacked them first, no matter that they violated our sovereignty and jailed one of our officers."

The baron nodded. "I left our men on alert and added patrols. I wanted to tell you personally, but I need to return to them promptly." He scooped up the whimpering Azor.

"This could impact our ability to reach a compromise. And, if hostilities break out..." Warner shook his head and frowned. "News of this will reach the captain's ears. It is best that I be up front and inform him of the circumstances. Any news of our Colonel Fairbanks?"

"No. But if our folks have those Yorkers, perhaps an exchange can be arranged before this gets out of hand." As he scratched Azor's head, the baron smiled. "Having a British officer—Captain Brehm—with us could prove advantageous."

Now Warner nodded. "Especially if this is settled before any higher-ranked British are involved. Send that civilian back with orders for them not to harm their prisoners and for the Yorkers to be brought here. I'll take care of everything here. Keep our men vigilant."

Back in camp, the sky streaked with charcoal clouds, von Steuben's orders were distributed. The civilian rider carried a letter signed by the baron ordering the captive Yorkers be brought to Bennington. Von Steuben sat with Azor on his lap, while he idly scratched the dog's chest as he considered his next move. He didn't have much time, as a rider arrived with urgent news: A militia regiment of Yorkers was spotted moving toward Bennington along the Walloomsac River.

"And so it begins," the baron uttered. He conferred with his trusted officers and developed a plan of engagement. He would split his forces. One captain would take a force north, along the river, concealing themselves along the low-lying riverbank; another force would travel east, with the intent of flanking the Yorkers. The baron would lead a frontal assault, engaging in battle once the first shots were fired.

—◦—

After dawn broke, the New York militia crossed the Little White Creek into disputed territory. The regiment easily forded the creek, its depth no more than boot-high after weeks without rain. They moved under ordered silence, marching in route step and not in unison so as not to give away that a large force was approaching. The way was clear, and they encountered no resistance, traveling unhindered. By noon, the force reached the Walloomsac River. Following its course would lead them straight into Bennington.

Clouds rolled in from the west, blocking the sun and bringing a welcomed release from the relentless sun of the days-long march. But as the afternoon wore on, the sky darkened. *A storm is approaching*, Griffith thought. *Perhaps the cover we need to free our kidnapped men without a fight.*

They traversed a short incline, bringing them well above the river to their left. The expedition crested the hill's peak and navigated the downslope. Griffith gazed again at the darkening clouds rolling in from the west. "Colonel," he whispered, "I don't like the looks of this." Griffith barely had time to finish his sentence before ear-splitting screams arose from behind them. He turned to see Green Mountain Rangers charging down the hill screaming with primal fury. The first shots cracked the air almost simultaneously. Several men fell, howling in pain.

Griffith leaped from his horse—*no use being an easy target*. He grabbed his leather case and crawled to the nearest fallen man. While musketballs whizzed over his head, he focused on the task at hand despite the chaos around him. *Where the devil did they come from?* Officers organized their men who returned fire, initially slowing the rangers' progress. As he wrapped the closest wounded man's leg with a cloth, attempting to stop the loss of blood, the sky flashed a brilliant white with a crack of thunder seconds later. He finished tying the cloth and edged his way to another man, freshly fallen. The first droplets of rain, big and heavy, crashed around him as he heard another round of fire. His Yorkers returned fire but now were confronted with an attack from two sides.

Thunder rumbled across the landscape. Griffith watched in horror as a horseman, his breeches stained bloody, his sword raised high, led the rangers screaming down the hill and toward him. This bloody apparition, with men charging with fixed bayonets, broke the Yorkers' resolve. Men turned and fled. They slipped and fell over one another to escape the onslaught. Many threw their weapons down and gave themselves up.

Griffith was the last to exit the field, busy attending to another wounded soldier. His horse was nowhere to be found, he ran after the fleeing militia. Griffith made it only a few steps into the forest before stumbling over a rotting tree. Hearing footsteps close by, he crouched in the undergrowth and peered under the log. Within a few seconds, Green Mountain Rangers were upon him. The first there pressed a bayonet against his chest. Griffith's heart pounded as rain dripped through the canopy, soaking him. He held his breath, bracing for the bayonet's thrust.

"Get up!" the ranger commanded. "You're one of them Yorkers, come to attack us. Thought you'd stroll in here and catch us unawares." Griffith felt the point of the bayonet against his skin. He stepped back. "Don't you bloody move," the ranger barked. "You look like an officer."

"I am," Griffith ventured. "But I'm a surgeon. I'm not here to fight. I'm here to treat any wounded." He thrust out his hand to shake his captor's hand. The ranger withdrew his musket. *That seems to have helped, for now*, Griffith thought. Then the man grabbed him, pulled him over the rotting log, and went through his pockets, pulling out a watch. Griffith's jaw tightened. *My father's watch.* The soldier held it to his ear. Satisfied that it was ticking, he pocketed it and turned to a fellow ranger coming up behind. "Take this prisoner back to camp." The second man pointed his bayonet at him, and Griffith walked off. "And don't harm him," the first ranger yelled after him. "He's a surgeon."

———◦———

Von Steuben watched his flanking forces depart. They moved in tight formations and quickly closed the distance to the Walloomsac River. *My training is paying dividends.* He moved his men forward, positioning them for his frontal attack on the approaching Yorkers. Von Steuben dismounted his horse. With a silent hand signal, von Steuben ordered Azor to stay. The dog obeyed, lying flat on its stomach in the grass. He moved forward on foot to the edge of a hill with his men. The first rumbles of thunder rolled over the mountains.

They didn't wait long. Before the echoes of the first shots stopped, the baron had his troops moving forward at double time. As they rounded a bend in the river, the Yorkers were 150 yards distant. The baron held his hand high—a command to hold fire. They awaited his arm to fall as a signal to fire. All eyes were on the baron's arm. With a swift motion, he swung his arm down as the sky flashed a brilliant white. The crack of thunder obscured the roar of the musket fire.

Prime and load, beat the drum command. Every ranger readied his musket. The baron led the men forward. The command to fire by unit traveled through the ranks as thunder rumbled across the landscape. The first droplets of rain pelted the field. Von Steuben shouted a command for all units to fire. *Before we lose the ability to fire in this damned rain!* The Green Mountain Rangers fired and were answered with the scream of return fire.

A searing pain tore through his thigh. Von Steuben tumbled to the ground. "I'm hit! *Verdammter scheisse!*" du Ponceau appeared at his side. "Help me up," von Steuben insisted. "Prop me against this tree. Get my horse, *gottverdammt!*"

Du Ponceau ran back for the baron's horse as the rain poured down, making firing a flintlock impossible. "Steel!" Von Steuben drew his sword and screamed the command through the downpour. "Fix bayonets!" the command echoed through the woods. Riding the baron's horse, du Ponceau leaped down as he arrived and helped him mount her. Von Steuben, his breeches stained bloody, his arm thrust forward, pointing his sword, led the men screaming toward the Yorker line.

Von Steuben watched his men chase the fleeing Yorkers with pride. His leg throbbed with every quick heartbeat. Pierre came up beside him, his face etched with worry.

"We best get you back to camp and a surgeon."

"*Nein!* Not until we finish them," von Steuben growled, wincing.

Chapter 6

A Diversion

Lucy had prepared dinner in Ira's home, as she had done often during the past months of staying with her brother. This evening, Ira brought Captain Brehm as a dinner guest. She carried several dishes from the separate brick kitchen that housed the massive fireplace for cooking to the dining table. As she made her final trip carrying a basket of fresh bread and churned butter, a rumble of thunder rolled across the hills.

Captain Brehm rose from his seat alongside her brother at the narrow dining table. "It is nice to see you, Mrs. Armistead."

"It is a pleasure to see you as well." Lucy smoothed an invisible wrinkle on the bone-color linen tablecloth. "Also, I'm grateful for the additional company. Ira has lately been all business or entirely mum." She glanced at her brother with a grin. They all sat at the narrow dining table.

The smell of the freshly baked bread was too much for Brehm to resist. He broke a piece off as steam rose from the interior. "This is delicious. It reminds me of Quebec." He smiled as he took another bite.

Lucy smiled in return, stealing a glance into his amber eyes. "I thought you might like it. Adelaide gave me the recipe as I so enjoyed it while we were in Quebec."

Brehm cut a piece of meat for his plate. "This meal looks delicious, Mrs. Armistead."

"It's one of Ira's favorites. Roasted venison wrapped in bacon."

"I can see why," Brehm said, having taken a bite.

"Thank you, Captain. I hope your discussions today were fruitful. Anything particularly interesting happen today?"

Brehm raised his eyebrows and looked at Ira, who nodded slightly. "Indeed. Today was out of the ordinary." Lucy leaned forward. "General von Steuben reported—"

"The baron was here?" Lucy interrupted.

"Yes," Brehm continued. "He felt it was important enough to deliver the news himself." Brehm told Lucy the news about Fairbanks's kidnapping and the retaliatory raid and abduction of the men from Albany.

"Why would the Yorkers risk this move now?" Lucy asked. "Your presence here is not a well-kept secret. You moved out of the Dewey Inn due to many prying ears. We're close enough to Albany that I'm sure some of the patrons hail from there. So it must be known in Albany that Vermont and Britain are in talks."

"To sabotage those talks," Ira said. "If we reach an agreement—" he looked at Brehm—"New York has no claim on us."

"All the more reason to join us," Brehm said, nodding to Ira. "Things like this wouldn't happen if Vermont were part of the British Empire." He paused. "We wouldn't *allow* them to happen." He tapped his finger on the table to emphasize the word.

Ira laughed. "You'll not get me to make a separate agreement with you this evening. This was supposed to be a convivial evening."

"This is all so enthralling," Lucy said. "What is to be done about it?"

"I was thinking," Brehm said between bites of venison. "It may be useful to have a British officer intercede on behalf of this kidnapped Vermonter. General Warner informed me that your baron sent for the New Yorkers abducted in response. Once they arrive, I can head to Albany and arrange an exchange. Of course, it means putting current discussions on hold until this is all worked out."

"The Yorkers entered our territory with the express intent to grab our colonel," Ira said. "While I can't condone his kinfolk's response, I understand their anger. But I'd like to avoid any more violence. I think the council would be grateful if you interceded."

A flash of lightning illuminated the interior of the room. An ear-splitting clap of thunder made Lucy jump from her seat. Rain pelted the roof and blew in the open window. Lucy closed the window, latching it shut, and lit several candles as illumination against the sudden darkness.

———◈———

The rain, though heavy, was brief. The wounded and captured Yorkers were brought to the hilltop headquarters. All told, there were thirty-four uninjured prisoners and nine wounded, along with four or five Yorkers killed in the skirmish. The rangers had suffered four injuries, with von Steuben's the most serious. The wounded prisoners were being treated by one of their own captured men.

"It throbs with every heartbeat," von Steuben said, his voice strained. He sat in his tent with his wounded leg propped up, Azor lying on the ground beside him.

"We sent a rider for the doctor in Bennington," du Ponceau responded. "I'd like you to get that taken care of sooner than waiting

for him, though." He frowned, looking at the blood-stained breeches.
"Let me take them off you."

The baron winced as du Ponceau unbuttoned them and attempted
to remove them. "No use, I'll need to cut them off." He reached for a
knife and made a cut above the wound.

The baron gritted his teeth as du Ponceau cut. "Careful, Pierre. I'd
rather keep the leg."

"You make a joke at a time like this? This needs to be taken care of,
Friedrich. I'm concerned for you."

"What's the alternative, Pierre? I'll await Dr. Fay."

"There's a captured officer treating the wounded Yorkers," du Ponceau said.

"And I should trust him? After we just defeated them?"

"I'm bringing him here. Let's see what he has to say." Du Ponceau
left the tent.

A few minutes later, he returned with the Yorker prisoner who
carried a leather case. "He says he's Lieutenant Caleb Griffith, New
York militia and a trained physician," du Ponceau said as he entered
the tent.

"I'm General von Steuben."

"I know who you are," Griffith said, allowing vitriol to seep into
his voice. "We all rejoiced when word first reached us that you were
coming to help train our Continental forces. Now," he shook his head
at all that had happened since last fall, "everything has changed."

"You and I are not enemies, or, at least, we should not be," von
Steuben said. "We had the same goal—freedom from the British. Here,
in the Vermont Republic, we still harbor that sentiment. I did my best
to help the Continentals in Boston, though that did not work as I had

hoped." He grimaced and closed his eyes.

Griffith shifted his focus to the wound. "Let me examine your leg," he said. It was more of a command than a request as he knelt beside the baron. Griffith probed the front thigh, then the back. "The ball appears to have cleanly passed through your leg. I can treat you if you'll allow me."

Von Steuben nodded. Du Ponceau let out an audible breath of relief.

Griffith opened his leather case. "I need some cloth," he said to du Ponceau, "and whiskey or rum if you have it." Du Ponceau exited the tent, returning a few minutes later with a linen shirt. He handed it to Griffith, then pulled a bottle of whiskey from the chest in the far corner of the baron's tent.

"Give him a drink." Griffith nodded to the baron. "He'll need it. The bleeding has stopped, thankfully. I won't need to cauterize it. Hand me the whiskey."

Du Ponceau widened his eyes but handed the bottle to Griffith, who immediately poured some on the top wound and splashed some on the exit wound. The baron yelped.

"What the hell are you doing?" shouted du Ponceau, stepping forward. Von Steuben waved him off.

"Something I learned in Scotland," Griffith said without looking up. "It seems to improve the healing process." He rummaged through his leather case, extracting a clear bottle with a viscous amber fluid. "Here it is. Tear some strips of cloth. I'll need to wrap his leg." Griffith opened the container and allowed some liquid to drop on the entry wound. After adding more liquid to cover the exit wound, he wrapped the leg with the linen cloth.

"What is that stuff?" du Ponceau asked.

"Honey," Griffith said. Du Ponceau gaped. "It's a trick I learned from the Oneida. It helps reduce infections, which is my main concern now. My advice is to rest that leg. If you put pressure on it, it may start to bleed again." Griffith stood up. "May I be excused to continue treating our men?"

The baron nodded. "Thank you, Lieutenant Griffith."

Captain Brehm had retrieved his horse from Ethan's fenced-in meadow. Now, a grim Brehm checked his horse's saddle and tightened the straps holding it. General Warner stood nearby.

"This skirmish complicates matters," Brehm said. "Word undoubtedly has reached Albany." He frowned as he packed a map of the area provided by Ethan and provisions for the road into his satchel.

"We were invaded," Warner responded. "I commended the baron for his defense in preventing them from reaching here. Lord knows what would have happened had they made it." His expression hardened. "I've ordered a regiment to be positioned around Bennington in case they intend to send another force."

Brehm nodded. "What word on the baron?"

"He remains with the troops while he recuperates from the bullet wound. Apparently, a physician among the captured Yorkers treated him." He rubbed the horse behind his ears and looked at Brehm. "What's your plan?"

"I ride for Albany and seek out the governor there. I have the authority of the British Crown behind me. These incursions must stop. From both sides, General. I cannot negotiate a truce if Vermont breaks it. Do you understand?"

Warner paused before answering. "Captain Brehm, Colonel Fairbanks's kidnapping elicited a natural response by his kinfolk. You know that was not an authorized raid by any means. But you have my word that I will reiterate that no offensive measures are undertaken."

"Thank you, General." Brehm mounted his horse.

"And Captain," Warner said, looking up at Brehm, "The Vermont Council meets to discuss our negotiations in light of these events."

Brehm sighed. "I'll send word after I've spoken with the governor." He shook the reins and ushered the horse into a trot.

———————•◦•———————

"Captain Brehm left this morning for Albany," Ira said to his sister over dinner that evening. "The council spent the day arguing over how all this impacts our negotiations. Several of the more militant members want to order his immediate departure."

"They won't send him away, will they?" Lucy asked, squinting with worry.

"I believe the captain has made a favorable impression on you. Yet Lucy, you must exercise caution. He's not from here. If we're not successful, there could be war." Ira pursed his lips. "It wasn't so long ago that they held Ethan prisoner."

"And I helped get him freed, did I not?"

Yes, you succeeded where I floundered, thought Ira. *Governor Haldimand chose wisely. The captain has been a worthy adversary. So what are his intentions for you, my dear sister? You've been your old self these past weeks, and for that, I am grateful. But is he using you to get to us? And if he is, you'll be devastated. But if his interest is sincere, you have a chance for happiness again.* "Yes, and I'm grateful for what you accomplished. Though the captain claims his part was but a small one in Ethan's release."

"Ethan tells a different story, you know that. The captain is far too humble to accept the credit. And yes, Ira, I have formed an attachment to him. He's kind, he converses with me as an equal, and he values my thoughts. No one aside from Elias has ever treated me that way." She swallowed hard upon uttering her late husband's name. "I shall always miss Elias, but I cannot remain in mourning forever. He would not wish me to live in perpetual sorrow. I've indulged in enough of that over the past year to last a lifetime."

"I fear for your heart should this end badly."

"I cannot know what Providence holds. But I must trust that happiness may yet be granted me again."

Ira nodded. "Providence indeed offers no certainties. These negotiations could well fail, and we may find ourselves at war."

"Then you must not let them fail. I could not bear it."

A stern-faced Brehm stood opposite Governor Jay, who remained behind his office desk with his fingers pressed against its surface, as the British officer pointed an accusing finger at him. Brehm had barged past the governor's secretary and into his office, confronting John Jay.

"Do I need to write General Sir Henry Clinton in New York and inform him it was under your orders the militia was sent to Vermont?" asked Brehm, his voice raised. "I wrote Governor Haldimand's letters to General Clinton myself. I know he ordered the cessation of militia activity against Vermont. You," he repeated for emphasis, almost shouting, "You disregarded that. And for what? To get back two kidnappers?"

The governor recoiled. "No!" he shouted back. "The Vermonters attacked us unprovoked. We were defending ourselves. That is expressly allowed."

"And what of Colonel Fairbanks?" Brehm shot back.

"Who? I know of no one by that name, sir."

"What? What do you mean? This entire affair is because you hold him captive. Your people kidnapped him from Vermont. That's what precipitated all this."

The governor opened his office door and yelled for his secretary. When the man appeared, he demanded, "Who is Colonel Fairbanks?"

"I don't know, sir."

"Find out. And quickly." Jay slammed the door after his secretary scurried out. "I seem to be missing some important information, Captain. Tell me what you know." He walked to the sideboard and reached for a crystal decanter. "First, I need a drink. Would you care for some brandy?"

Brehm nodded. Jay motioned to one of the two chairs facing the desk and poured two glasses. Handing Brehm one of them, he sat in the other chair, turning it to face Brehm. Brehm told of the Fairbanks's kidnapping as Baron von Steuben had related it to him. The governor listened intently as the story unfolded, taking several sips of brandy. When Brehm concluded his account, Jay swallowed the rest of his drink in one gulp and sighed.

"If it is as you relate, I take full responsibility. We shall see soon enough. There may be more that neither of us knows." He cast his eyes to the floor and shook his head. Looking up again, he continued, "I want our men back, both the captured militia and the two men you're accusing of kidnapping."

"That's why I'm here. With the full weight of British authority behind me," he bluffed, not having any authority to negotiate with New York. "Mark my words," he looked Jay squarely in the eyes, "if Colonel Fairbanks has been harmed, New York will pay dearly."

Chapter 7

Chess

Lucy moved her bishop, setting a challenge to the queen.

"You've improved since we last played," Ethan said.

Two sconces in Ethan's parlor illuminated the chessboard on the small table between them. The two were alone and took the opportunity to play chess for the first time since Ethan's return.

"This is a beautiful set, Lucy."

"Thank you. I first saw it in Quebec." She looked up at Ethan after considering her next move. "You know, it reminded me of you—all those evenings after Da died when you kept me occupied. You were—are—a father to me. I cannot thank you enough." Her eyes glistened in the candlelight.

"And I was proud of you. I still am. I'm just sorry I wasn't here for you after Elias…" He broke off.

"It wasn't your fault, Ethan. How could it be?"

"I could have signed that loyalty oath and been out sooner."

"That was still after…"

"And the baby. I didn't even know." Ethan brushed at his eyes with his sleeve.

"I've done enough crying for the two of us. I'm done. I'm looking to the future now. For a long time, I could never imagine there was a future."

"It makes me happy to hear you say that. Ira told me how you blossomed in Quebec and about a nascent romance between you and Captain Brehm."

"I don't know if I'd call it a romance. I've grown fond of him, though."

"I've seen his eyes light up when he looks at you." Even in the candlelight, Ethan saw Lucy's cheeks turn rosy. "He has made a favorable impression upon me since my return as well. He's an honorable man." He looked directly into Lucy's eyes. "He's also a soldier. A soldier in an army that could overrun Vermont. Remember whose side he's on."

Lucy cast her eyes back to the chessboard. "Your move, Ethan."

Ethan considered the pieces and moved his rook, setting up his next move. Lucy quickly took his queen.

"The captain is in Albany now, working on our behalf. Something he needn't have volunteered for," Lucy said.

"I expect he thinks it will help him in our negotiations. He's a shrewd negotiator and doesn't give anything away without first calculating."

Lucy examined the chess board again. "I think you misjudge him." She paused for a moment, determined to change the subject from her interest in Brehm. "How did the council discussions go today?"

Ethan frowned. "The Yorkers' attack didn't soften any hearts." Looking at the board again, he smiled. "You still jump into moves I see." He moved his knight. "Check."

Lucy considered the board, shook her head, and flicked her king over, conceding the game. "Shall we play another? I've missed this."

Ethan smiled and nodded, beginning to reset the board. "The council is split," he told her. "Some want to take a harder stance. More guarantees against attack, or the commitment that British soldiers would defend us. There are a few who want to cut off negotiations completely." His brow furrowed. "That likely would lead to soldiers pouring in from Quebec."

"Where does General Warner stand?" Lucy knew that Seth Warner's word carried significant sway. This was especially true now after his rangers, under the command of the man he personally recruited, had handily defeated a Yorker force.

"He wants to continue negotiations under the same expectations as before: independence."

Lucy moved a pawn two spaces forward. "I agree with him. Otherwise, we'll get swallowed up."

"We're going to need a more convincing argument for continued independence than what we've been able to muster so far. Your captain has countered every proposal."

"Then guide him into making a proposal. What better way than to plant an idea in his head and make him think it's his own?"

"Somehow, Lucy, I get the feeling you've done that before."

She gave him a wry smile. "Your move, Ethan."

———— ❦ ————

Brehm returned to Bennington two days later, accompanied by Samuel Fairbanks. He had left the New York governor with a written pledge that their captured militia members, along with the two abductees, would be set free and allowed to return to Albany. *My return with Fairbanks will create goodwill with the council*, thought Brehm. *This only increases my chances of success.*

Their arrival in Bennington brought out almost the entire town. Lucy heard the commotion from Ira's house. She walked the short distance across the common to where the crowds gathered, arriving as Brehm and Fairbanks rode to the Dewey Inn. With a broad smile, Fairbanks waved to the assembled crowd. Huzzahs rang out from the spectators. Captain Brehm dismounted and handed the reins to a stable hand he recognized. Lucy watched as he said something inaudible to Fairbanks, who also dismounted. They walked into the inn, and the crowd dispersed, some heading into the tavern for gossip, others returning to their chores.

He's headed into the council session, no doubt, Lucy thought. *I think I'll make one of Ira's favorite meals. He's likelier to linger over it, so I can hear more of what happened today.* She headed home to prepare dinner.

Upon entering the inn, Brehm and Fairbanks were escorted to the council meeting room on the second floor, where General Warner and Ira Allen waited to greet them. The council members jockeyed to shake Fairbanks's hand, and Brehm was repeatedly thanked. Standing before the assembled, Ira Allen shouted for everyone to take their seats.

"Captain Brehm, it is with great delight that I thank you, on behalf of our grateful republic, for the safe return of our Colonel Fairbanks," Ira began. The room erupted into cheers, and Ira again waved for the room to quiet down. "The people of Vermont will remember your efforts on our behalf for a long time. For the past few days, our rangers have been alert for additional incursions by New York. Your return with the colonel today brings hope that we can secure a peace with New York and achieve an honorable agreement with you on behalf of the British Empire." More cheers erupted, but they were not as boisterous as before. "Captain Brehm, please fill us in on your successful mission to Albany and your discussions."

Brehm spoke at length about his meetings with New York governor John Jay. He told the council of the governor's claim that troops were sent under mistaken information. Brehm assured the council that British authority remained over the militia and that no further incursions would occur. Finally, he informed them of the agreements established for Fairbanks's return. General Warner caught Ira Allen's eye and raised his eyebrows. Ira nodded in response.

"Captain," Ira said, "there is still much for the council to discuss. We would like Colonel Fairbanks to remain here for further discussions. We'll continue our discussions tomorrow. Thank you again."

Ira clasped Brehm's hand and escorted him out of the meeting room. Standing outside the inn, Brehm let out an exhausted sigh and contemplated his next move. *There is much to do, and I have letters to write.* He headed to his quarters in Ethan Allen's home. There, he wrote to Sir General Henry Clinton about the situation—and its resolution.

Brehm sat at his writing desk, quill in hand, as Ethan Allen entered the study. Brehm rose to greet him. "Mr. Allen, it is good to see you again.

"I heard you were back—and with Colonel Fairbanks as well! Word reached General von Steuben's camp while I was there."

"How does he fare? Is he recovering?"

"He's as stubborn as ever." Ethan grinned as he recalled the colorful mix of curses the baron had muttered every time he tried to move too much. *Serves him right*, thought Ethan. *The doctor ordered him to rest anyway.* "He refuses to leave camp to convalesce. Says he must remain with his rangers."

"From what I know of him, it doesn't surprise me."

"As I left the stable just now," Ethan jerked his head toward where he had left his horse in the hands of his stable boy, "I saw Ira returning home. I'm headed over there now."

"May I walk with you?" Brehm asked. "I've sat too long writing and could do with a walk."

Ethan tilted his head and raised his eyebrows. "This wouldn't have anything to do with my sister making supper there, would it?" His eyes held Brehm's before his mouth curved into a smile. "Come, keep me company."

As they walked alongside the stone walls marking the edge of Ethan's property, the path worn bare from years of foot traffic, Brehm's gaze drifted to the angry clouds gathering on the western horizon. "Looks like we're in for more rain."

Ethan looked in that direction and shrugged. "But it won't be here until morning."

Lucy greeted them at Ira's door with a gentle smile, her apron dusted with flour. "He's in the parlor," she said with a nod in that direction. "Not very talkative."

They found Ira seated in his wingback chair, swirling a glass of whiskey and frowning. He greeted his brother with a subdued "Ethan." To Brehm he gave a curt "Captain" and averted his eyes.

"Rough day?" Ethan asked quietly.

"Just tired. It's been a long day. We should talk, though." Ira's eyes flickered between Brehm and his brother. "Privately."

Brehm hesitated, wondering if he should return to Ethan's home, until Lucy's voice came from behind him. "Perhaps a game of chess in the garden, Captain Brehm?" she asked with a lilt. "The sun won't be setting for a while. Why don't we leave my brothers to talk?" She wiped her hands on her apron.

"One game, perhaps. Thank you." With a nod to Ethan, he followed Lucy to the garden.

They sat on benches across from each other, flanking the wooden table on which the chess set he had gifted her rested. Fragrance from the nearby late-blooming lavender plants wafted over them. Lucy had removed other blooms weeks earlier to dry for medicinal needs.

"Every game I play on this, I think of you," Lucy said shyly.

"I'm honored to hear that. I only wish we had time to play more often. I have enjoyed the matches we've played."

Lucy opened by moving her king's pawn. "Captain, can you tell me about your discussions in Albany?"

He mirrored Lucy and moved his own king's pawn. "What is it that you'd like to know?"

"The Yorkers. I don't trust them. From what I know they seem to be ... vengeful." Her gaze lingered on the board and she brought her knight out.

"Well, most people kept to themselves, though that may have been due to my uniform. Otherwise, their leadership was much as I expected. They acceded to British military authority. Their new governor was exceedingly gracious, especially after discovering his people initiated the conflict." Brehm again mirrored her move, bringing out his knight. "We concluded our negotiations fairly quickly. Once he released the colonel to me, I gave him my assurances that his captured militia—and the abducted kidnappers—would be released. I also ordered that there be no additional attacks. And I've informed General Clinton in New York of the particulars."

"I'm sure they'll be happy this incident wasn't worse."

A breeze rustled through the nearby maple trees, and a few of their leaves blew across the garden, a stark reminder of autumn approaching. "Yes indeed, there are more pressing matters," Brehm agreed.

"I've never been to New York territory. I never had a need. What was Albany like? I hear it's bigger than Bennington, though not as large as Quebec City."

"The town itself is larger, with beautiful rolling hills and farms surrounding it." He gazed at Lucy's face. "Though having spent time here, I prefer this area and the views here."

Lucy blushed and looked down at the chessboard. "When will you meet with the council again?"

"I will continue our discussions with the council tomorrow. When we returned this afternoon, they were eager to speak with Colonel Fairbanks. Hopefully, the council will be as eager as I am to reach an agreement."

"And if not?" Lucy met his eyes. "What happens then?" She clenched the pawn she had just taken.

Brehm removed his hand from his bishop, frowning. "I'll be forced to report back to Governor Haldimand that I was unsuccessful in returning Vermont to the king." He sighed and shook his head. *What happens then, indeed*, he thought. *Another war? And the possibility I will lose her forever?* "We must reach an agreement. Otherwise," his voice trailed off. He looked back at the board moving his bishop.

Lucy understood his hesitation. "How many men would you need to suppress Vermont?" she said softly. "It's likely more than you either can or are willing to commit. And then, how long would you need to stay? Longer than you probably think you need." She moved her rook across the board. "Your move."

Captain Brehm looked at the board again, contemplating Lucy's words. He reached for his queen but pulled his hand back. *Am I the one who'll bring destruction to Vermont? I couldn't bear to see this land and people devastated by war.* He took his eyes off the board and gazed into Lucy's eyes. "What would you have us do instead? Vermont was part of the empire, and the king expects us to be reunited." He looked back at the board and moved his queen diagonally.

Lucy studied the board, then back at Brehm. "Perhaps this little area with little economic or strategic significance should not be where you focus your efforts. A protracted conflict with Vermont would harm everyone, except perhaps the French." A corner of her mouth lifted. "However, Captain, imagine the possibilities of a natural ally on Quebec's border. It could allow you to deploy troops to other, more pressing areas, opening up new strategic opportunities." She reached for her bishop and moved it diagonally across the board. "Check."

"Why, Mrs. Armistead, I think you've distracted me from our game. Checkmate in two, I believe?" He flicked his finger on his king, knocking it over. "Well done."

A somber-faced Ethan emerged from Ira's home into the garden and suggested to Brehm that they head back. The walk back was unusually quiet. Brehm was too preoccupied with replaying his talk with Lucy to mind the silence.

Later that evening, Ethan was sitting in his parlor contemplating the rum in his glass when there was a knock at his door. His brother entered.

"Is the captain here?"

Ethan nodded to the drawing room, just as Brehm emerged.

Ira swallowed hard. "Captain Brehm, I need to discuss with you the council's decision."

Brehm waved toward the drawing room. "Shall we?" They stepped into the room. "I was just writing a letter to Governor-General Haldimand about the successful negotiations leading to Colonel Fairbanks's release."

Ira frowned. "Indeed. I want you to know that I am personally thankful for your actions." He cast his eyes to the floor. "I only wish that the council felt the same."

A chill ran through Brehm as he stared at Ira in silence, steeling himself.

Ira hesitated, then shook his head. "I tried—I tried to no avail." He looked at Brehm. "The council will not release the Yorkers. They intend to try them for kidnapping."

Brehm took a deep breath and straightened to his full height. "Why?" His voice grew louder. "Have I not freed Colonel Fairbanks?"

"It's not that. They feel the perpetrators deserve to be punished."

Brehm's face flushed with anger. "You dishonor me, Mr. Allen. I gave my word to Governor Jay that his men would be returned unharmed. Now you threaten to try them?"

"What would you have had me do?" Ira threw his hands wide. "I am but one voice among the council. Would that I could change their minds."

"If my word cannot be trusted, what am I doing here? I returned from Albany with Fairbanks. It is you who has not held up to the bargain I negotiated. You must release the Yorkers."

"You know I alone cannot make that decision."

"Then you must convince the council."

"Have you not heard me? I argued with them. There's a majority that feels a trial must occur."

"I cannot accept that answer. I will not accept it."

"There's nothing more I can do." Ira looked away.

Brehm stormed out of the house.

Chapter 8

Shattered Pieces

When Brehm awoke, it had already been raining for some time. The dirt path visible from his window looked like a small stream. He boiled water in a pot suspended within the parlor fireplace. He steeped the tea from the dwindling supply he'd brought from Quebec. It was almost all gone now. *I might have to switch to that godforsaken coffee they drink—if I stay any longer.* He trembled. *Is that the morning's damp chill? Or my desire to stay here longer?* He poured the tea into a cup and wrapped his hands around his traveling mug, enjoying the warmth. *I cannot stay. The council has made it impossible with their intransigence. My duty is to my king. I shall head back to Quebec City for consultations with Governor Haldimand. Autumn is approaching. Better to head back now if we are to prepare for war.* He frowned. *How can I do that? How can I bring war to Lucy? Damn them! Damn them for forcing this upon me.*

He sat at the small dining table and sipped his tea, organizing his thoughts. *Logic, Brehm. What are my options? One, I stay here and convince the council to adhere to my agreement with Governor Jay. Will it work? Ira made clear last night that the council was adamant. He had attempted to do the same in vain. Do I trust his word?* He took another sip of tea. "I do," he muttered. *He's kept his word throughout. I don't think my protestations will make a difference. Option two? I head back to Quebec. I've already been here longer than I anticipated. If I am honest, I've delayed to spend more time with Lucy. Do I dare think there could be a future with her if I bring war to her people?* Brehm stared into the cup and swirled the remaining liquid. "Damn it!" he shouted and threw the cup of tea into the fireplace, shattering it into pieces, his head slumping into his hands.

———◦——

The baron lay in his tent, a more comfortable bed having been brought to the field because he'd refused to leave his troops. The sound of rain hitting the tent and the distant rumble of thunder filled the air. Azor lay curled up at the bottom of the bed. The dog raised his head as General Warner entered the tent.

"I hope I'm not disturbing your rest," Warner said, shaking the rain from his regimental.

"No. Where's Pierre?" asked the baron.

"Outside. He'll be in." Warner reached down and scratched Azor's head. The dog lifted his head to give Warner a better angle. Warner looked at the baron's leg, bandaged in fresh linen. "How is it?"

"*Gut,*" he said, adding in English, "I will live." *But I should be out in the field with my men,* he thought. "*Du siehst besorgt aus.*"

Warner raised his eyebrows just as Pierre's voice came behind him, "'You look worried,'" he said.

Warner chuckled. "It shows?"

"We've worked together long enough," the baron said, with Pierre translating. "Pull up a chair. Talk to me."

Warner grabbed a chair and sat down. Azor vigorously shook his head, yawned, and curled by the baron's bandaged leg.

"The council insists on a trial for the kidnappers. They won't exchange them as negotiated by Captain Brehm. And the captain rode for Quebec this morning." He sighed. "We need to plan for the worst. I fear the British will pour across our northern border." He rubbed his temples. "We were so close to a breakthrough. This damned attack hardened some hearts."

"Why do you expect an attack from the north? I wouldn't. We're surrounded now that the Continentals surrendered. Why not attack from New York? Or Connecticut? I wouldn't limit this to troops from Quebec."

Warner's eyes narrowed, and he stroked his chin. He nodded and said, "You're right, of course." *The council is being short-sighted*, Warner thought. *The baron has us better trained, but we'll never match their manpower.* "Let's review our strengths and where we need to shore up."

General Warner and Baron von Steuben began planning as the distant thunder grew louder. They spent the rest of the afternoon establishing plans for the general defense of the Vermont Republic.

———◈———

Ira visited his brother after the day's council session. They sat facing each other in Ethan's parlor, each ensconced in a wingback chair, the blueberry-colored upholstery of the arms worn, and holding a glass of amber brandy. The thunderstorms now over, the last rays of the sun stole through breaks in the clouds to shine through the windows. A small fire burned in the fireplace to ward off the damp air.

"They're still insisting on the trial," Ira said. "We had no luck convincing them it's a bad idea."

Ethan breathed in the aroma of the brandy before responding. "Captain Brehm left midmorning," Ethan said, the corners of his mouth downturned. "Lucy has been all tears. I only left her a short while ago after she fell asleep."

"I'll head home shortly. I'd rather she not be alone. But I came to see you first for a reason."

Ethan's eyebrows shot up, but he remained silent.

"They want you to defend the kidnappers in the trial," Ira said.

Ethan's arms involuntarily spread apart in astonishment. The only word that his mouth could form was, "Why?"

"Because of your background. You fought alongside the Yorkers before our independence." Ira frowned before continuing, "And you were held by the British. I surmise that some figure you may want to use this to exact some revenge on them."

"There are others more qualified," Ethan protested. *And I'll be despised for defending them.*

"Exactly. Do you think they want them acquitted? The faction in control doesn't want our negotiations with the crown to succeed. They think Seth and the baron have our rangers prepared to defend against a British invasion. I couldn't convince them we'd end up fighting along multiple fronts—not just on our northern border."

"So they expect me to fail," Ethan sat back abruptly, his jaw tightening. *The stakes are too high to fail, both for Vermont—and Lucy.*

"I recognize that look," Ira said. "Determination. Ferocity." Ira broke into a smile. "You're going to do this, aren't you?"

"I will. I am. They ought to be careful what they wish for." Ethan smirked. "When are they setting the trial?"

"The full council will hear the arguments."

"When?"

"Four days hence."

Ethan nodded his head and sighed. "I better get to work then."

———————◆———————

Eleven men of the Vermont Council sat in their well-worn wooden Windsor chairs arranged in two rows. General Warner sat next to Colonel Fairbanks, off to one side. A stern-faced Ethan Allen sat alone on the opposite side. The two accused stood at the front, the late-morning sun shining through the high windows, basking them in light.

Jonas Fay, the twelfth member of the Council and acting as prosecutor, stood before the assembled members. Tall and lean, with keen gray eyes, the forty-year-old physician wore a powdered wig on his head. "These two men, Mr. Henry Hawkins and Mr. Joseph Turner, stand accused of illegally entering the Vermont Republic with the intent to commit grievous crimes of theft, assault, and abduction of a prominent member of our community. This is a crime that shattered the delicate peace between New York and our republic. Colonel Fairbanks sits with us today, but the outcome could have been worse. You shall hear the heinous details from the victim himself, and I will bring witnesses to corroborate his account." He walked toward the council members, then stopped. "The evidence will show the defendants planned and executed a deliberate act of abduction with the intent to impress Colonel Fairbanks as a private in the New York militia against his will."

Fay paused to allow them to absorb the gravity of the charges. "You will hear from witnesses who heard these men"—he pointed at the defendants—"brag in public about the colonel's capture. The evidence will show a clear picture of the defendant's guilt." Jonas Fay smiled smugly as he stared at Ethan Allen. "The evidence is so clear that you will have no option but to return a guilty verdict." Fay returned to his seat.

Ethan Allen stood. "Gentleman, I am here to defend these men unjustly accused of these crimes." There was murmuring among the council members. General Warner sat upright in his chair as Fairbanks fidgeted. Ethan held up his hand until the murmuring subsided. "Not because there wasn't a crime committed—undoubtedly there was—but because the men who stand before you are not guilty. You know my history and the time I've spent away from my beloved Vermont, imprisoned by the British. During that time, I came to believe even more strongly that our republic should be forever independent of the influence of New York. Yet today, I stand before you to defend these Yorkers. Why? Because it's the right thing to do. It's the right thing to do as they are innocent of the crimes they are charged with. And I intend to bring witnesses who prove their innocence." Head held high, Ethan sat down.

The first witness for the prosecution was a carpenter who had been on his way to Fairbanks home to deliver a chest of drawers. He testified that as his wagon turned a bend in the road to Fairbanks home, he'd seen two men, cloaked in dark shirts, toss Fairbanks, his hands tied behind his back, over the back of a horse before they rode away.

Ethan stood, paused, then walked to the seated witness. "Tell us, did you see any distinguishing marks on the abductors' faces?"

"No."

"And why not? You stated you were close enough to see that Colonel Fairbanks was the victim."

"Their faces were covered with cloth."

"So you cannot place either of these men"—Ethan pointed at the accused—"at the scene of the abduction."

"No, but—"

"But what? You testified that you sought help when you saw what was going on. Isn't that so? Your interaction was limited to that brief interlude. And you cannot know these are the men that were there." He turned to the seated council. "No further questions for this witness."

Samuel Fairbanks was called to testify. He recounted masked men bursting into his home, his wife screaming, and being accosted by the intruders who tied his hands behind his back. He described the journey, how they'd draped him over the back of a horse on his stomach, each gallop of the horse pressing the breath out of him. How he heard muffled voices when they stopped, and how he was then dragged, gagged, and hurled onto the hard bed of a wagon, bales of wool atop him preventing any escape. As he was thrown into the cell, he said, the first person he saw was one of the defendants, and pointed directly at him.

"Colonel Fairbanks," Ethan stood in front of the seated man. "A harrowing tale indeed. You say the first person you saw when you were thrown into a cell was this defendant?" He pointed to Mr. Hawkins.

"He held the keys to the cell," Fairbanks recalled.

"So he was already there when you were dragged into the jail?"

Fairbanks hesitated. "I guess so."

"Therefore, he could not have been one of the men that abducted you, could he?"

"I don't know," Fairbanks mumbled.

"That's all the questions I have for Colonel Fairbanks."

Next up was the ranger who'd first spotted the men in the Albany tavern. He testified about overhearing the defendants bragging about holding Fairbanks captive.

Ethan Allen once again stood. "Your clandestine surveillance in Albany is truly remarkable. That you found men claiming to hold Colonel Fairbanks even more remarkable. Please tell us what you heard them say."

"They were laughing about having the colonel as a prisoner."

"Do you recognize the man whose voice you heard?"

The ranger pointed at one of the defendants. "I never forget a face. It was him," the ranger said, a flush rising in his cheeks.

Ethan Allen looked at the council members. "Let it be recorded that the witness pointed at Mr. Hawkins, defendant." He addressed the ranger again. "And do you recall his exact words?"

The ranger took a deep breath and closed his eyes. "I heard a loud voice laughing, then he said, 'You boys wrapped him up tighter than those bales of wool.'"

"'You boys.'" Ethan nodded his head in agreement. "'You boys' means he referenced other people." Ethan turned to the assembled members. "And he excluded himself. I submit to you that this defendant is not an abductor. This ranger's testimony exonerates him."

Jonas Fray jumped from his seat, shouting, "No! He may have been lying."

"Among friends?" Ethan retorted. "When he had no reason to believe any non-Yorkers were about? I think not!"

The eleven other council members leaned in and whispered to each other. Ethan walked over to the accused men and turned back to the ranger. "And what about this man?" He pointed to the second defendant. "You stated you never forget a face. Was he in Mr. Hawkins's group?" The man's eyes darted from Ethan to the ranger.

The ranger stared at the second man, examining his features. Finally, he lowered his eyes and mumbled, "He was not."

"What was that?" Ethan asked. "I couldn't hear you from over here."

The ranger cleared his throat. "He was not at that table."

Ethan stood in front of the council. "He was not at the table," he said softly. Then he raised his voice and pointed at the second defendant. "Mr. Turner was not at Mr. Hawkins's table. And," he said, stabbing at the air with his hand, "Mr. Hawkins did not abduct Colonel Fairbanks." He turned to Jonas Fay. "The prosecution's case is built on vapor and assumptions." Ethan stood in front of the seated council. "In fact, no witnesses have been presented that place Mr. Hawkins or Mr. Turner anywhere near the sovereign soil of the Republic of Vermont. These men are innocent!"

—⦿—

"You should have seen Ethan!" Ira paced the parlor of his home, too excited to sit. "It was a masterful performance. The council had no choice but to acquit them. A few were reluctant but could not hold out against the evidence." He stopped and looked at his sister. "After they were released a group of rangers escorted them to the border."

Lucy's hands fidgeted on her lap. "A week too late! Captain Brehm would still be here if they hadn't insisted on this trial. And where does this leave us?"

"With a chance."

"A chance for what?" Lucy's voice was laced with despair. "For war? For the destruction of our homes? Our freedoms?"

Ira sighed and sat down next to Lucy, shoulders slumped. "Lucy, I'm sorry. I was so excited with what Ethan did."

"I actually thought I could be happy again." She buried her face in her hands. "Now, I can't even imagine it. Theodore is our enemy." Tasting the bitterness of those words, she swallowed hard.

"I'm sorry I couldn't convince the captain to stay. I did try. Both Ethan and I tried."

Lucy lifted her head. "He said the same thing, you know. Rode to the house to say goodbye. His last words to me still echo in my mind: I'm sorry. I have to go." She looked down at her hands. "I wanted to hug him, stop him from leaving. But he never got off his horse and just rode off." She looked Ira in the eyes, the weight of the memory etched on her face. "Ethan saw me collapse right there in the yard."

They sat in silence for a moment.

"There were side conversations I overheard," Ira finally said, his voice soft. "Talk of sending another delegation to Quebec."

Quebec? Could there still be a chance? Lucy's eyes lit up. "Will they send you?"

"It should be me if they send a delegation."

"You can't wait to be asked. You need to lead it. You're the one who persuaded Governor Haldimand to send Captain Brehm for negotiations."

"I think you may have had something to do with that as well," Ira said, allowing himself a small smile.

"You need to go, and quickly, before the weather turns. You're only a week behind him." Lucy leaned toward her brother, her eyes pleading. "I should accompany you. No one will question it."

"I'm sure there will be discussions about it tomorrow."

"There's no time to waste. Can you line up support tonight? Have some discussions with other council members? Some must be at Dewey Tavern." Lucy stood up. "You should go now. The council must send you," she insisted, ushering Ira out the door to plan.

Governor John Jay had gathered several aides in his office, including the recently returned Caleb Griffith and his attorney general, Egbert Benson. The lanky and prematurely gray Benson had schemed to take the governorship when the prior governor fled after Congress's surrender. Failing in that, he remained as attorney general. The repatriated New Yorkers, Henry Hawkins and Joseph Turner, were being questioned about their trial in Vermont. The freed men had completed walking through Ethan Allen's pre-trial discussions with them, the development of their defense, and what transpired during the trial.

Jay stood up, prompting the others to do the same, and held out his hand. "Thank you for the account of the trial, Mr. Turner, Mr. Hawkins. You had a capable defense from Mr. Allen. I'm sure that Captain Brehm was relieved that you were freed. That was part of my agreement with him when we released their Colonel Fairbanks to his custody."

"Captain Brehm, sir?" Hawkins asked.

"The British officer in Bennington," Jay replied.

"Oh," Hawkins said. "We never saw him. I didn't even know his name until you just mentioned it."

Jay cocked his head. "He didn't attend the trial?"

"No, sir. Just before our trial, I overheard our guards speaking about a British officer. They said he stormed off back to Quebec."

Jay's expression sharpened. "Did you overhear anything else about Captain Brehm, either of you?"

"No," both Turner and Hawkins said. "But one guard said their rangers were preparing in case Quebec forces attack," Hawkins continued.

"Anything more?" Jay pressed.

Hawkins shook his head. "No."

"Are you sure? Anything, no matter how trivial you may think it."

This time, Turner answered, shaking his head. "No, sir. The person we spoke with the most was Mr. Allen. And he never mentioned Captain Brehm."

Jay pressed his lips together, nodding slowly. "Thank you, gentlemen. That will be all for now."

After they left the office, Jay once again sat at his desk. His eyes shifted between his two aides before settling on Caleb Griffith. "Lieutenant Griffith, what do you make of Captain Brehm's sudden departure?"

"Had to be a fierce disagreement for him to leave so abruptly," Griffith mused. "They made a liar out of the captain—duped him, maybe—by holding our men for trial after he negotiated their return."

"And he left before the trial," Benson said. "So he wasn't aware they were freed." He leaned forward in his chair. "And our men overheard their guards say there's concern the British could attack."

"That could be a fortunate turn for us," Jay said, growing animated.

"Let the British army do the work of driving them into submission. New York will then affirm our sovereignty over that land."

"It's a shame we can't help make that happen," Griffith interjected.

"I wonder..." Jay whispered, his gaze distant. "What if we could drive an even deeper wedge between Vermont and Quebec?"

"What are you thinking?" Griffith asked.

A sly smile crossed Jay's face. "Suppose we spread rumors that the French are moving to support Vermont?"

Griffith's eyes lit up. "The British are in constant fear the French are going to retake Quebec," he said. "We bloody hell have to keep an eye on our frontier against them." He frowned momentarily. "If Benjamin Franklin had succeeded in gaining French support, maybe all this would have played out differently." He shook his head. "I like the idea. We can make the British think they've been made the fool by Vermont."

"And spur them into action," Jay concluded.

"And I know the perfect contacts that would spread that story and make sure it gets to British military commanders," Griffith said.

Chapter 9

Reunion

Quebec City remained almost exactly as Lucy remembered it, except the weather was now colder. *At least the odor isn't as strong as in summer*, thought Lucy as she, Ira, and two other Vermonters rode through Lower Town. *Yesterday's rain helps as well.* "Do you think we'll have any issues getting into Upper Town? We don't have any passes or letters of introduction as we had before."

"I'm sure they'll let us in. I can't imagine the governor-general not wanting to hear why we're back." Ira said, but his expression betrayed his optimism.

Lucy pulled the hood of her red wool cloak over her head to ward off the cold drizzle that had started. *I have my doubts, but we shall see shortly.* The scent of freshly baked bread reached Lucy even before they rode past the Boulangerie Demange. Lucy smiled, the aroma and the clip-clop of the horses' hooves on the cobblestones bringing back happy memories.

Lucy's stomach fluttered as they rode up the inclined street to the massive stone Palais Gate, where they were curtly greeted by a red-headed guard. The group all dismounted their horses to present their two letters to the guard: the first addressed to Governor Haldimand, the second to Captain Brehm. The guard disappeared into the guard-house.

"This wait is interminable," Ira muttered.

The guard reappeared by himself, carrying the letters. "No admittance to Upper Town without authorization, and you have none."

"But our letters—"

"Here they are," the guard said, holding the letters out for Ira.

"Can they be delivered to the governor and Captain Brehm?" Ira pressed.

"You must go through official channels." The guard thrust the letters toward Ira again. Ira's jaw tightened, but he said nothing as he snatched the letters.

As they rode back to Lower Town, Lucy slumped in her saddle. She shivered as the cold dampness penetrated her bones.

"Where do we go now?" Ira asked, echoing Lucy's thoughts.

"I saw a sign advertising rooms for let," Lucy said. "Near the bakery we passed." *And where I can be on the lookout for Adelaide.*

"Official channels," Ira fumed. "What is more official than the military? If his superior officer had presented himself, we probably could have convinced him to have the letters delivered. Now I'll need to seek out the magistrate. And it'll likely take longer."

Their rented rooms were clean but sparse. Each had a bed, a few shelves, a writing desk, and an earthenware chamber pot. The sand-colored walls were peeling in spots. Lucy insisted on the smaller of the rooms, as it had a window overlooking the street opposite Boulangerie Demange. When Ira and his delegation went to seek the magistrate's office, Lucy took the opportunity to purchase stationery and writing implements. She stared at the blank page, hesitating for a moment. *Do I put on paper the yearnings of my heart?* She closed her eyes and imagined him reading it. Then she opened her eyes and began to write.

Dear Theodore,

I hesitate in writing you in fear that you may not respond. But I could not have traveled all this way without reaching out to you. You must know that I am here in Quebec City, along with my brother Ira. While he travels on official business for the Vermont Council, I am here because I miss you so. Your sudden departure left me bereft, Theodore, and the weight of your absence grows heavier with every heartbeat. I long for your presence with every breath. I know you have feelings for me that you do not dare express.

You and I are on opposing sides now, but that does not have to remain so. I hold onto hope—hope that we can find a way forward, not just for ourselves, but for Vermont and the Crown.

Your end of the agreement with New York was fulfilled. The men from Albany have been returned, and no barriers remain to continue your negotiations. Please, let us meet again, not as enemies, but as partners in this uncertain time. I beg you to grant us an audience and to intercede on our behalf with Governor Haldimand.

I pray that this letter finds you well and that I will again hear your voice. I do so miss you.

Your faithful servant,
Lucy

She folded the letter, pressed some wax on it, and tucked it in her bodice just as Ira returned.

The next few days fell into a routine: Ira and the delegates would wait at the magistrate's office for a meeting; Lucy would purchase fresh bread at Demange, then sit by the window in her room watching for Adelaide's carriage to pull in front of the bakery.

On the third day, Lucy began to despair. *What if Adelaide isn't here any longer? Perhaps her husband was transferred elsewhere or sent back to England.* As these thoughts coursed through her mind, a burgundy carriage stopped in front of the bakery, and a woman stepped from it. Lucy hurried down the stairs and across the square, stopping only to gather herself before stepping through the door into the bakery.

"Adelaide!" Lucy cried out.

Adelaide turned. Her face changed from startled to exuberant as she recognized Lucy. They rushed toward each other and embraced.

"Lucy, this is so unexpected. My word! How are you?" Adelaide held her at arms' length. "How is it that you're here? My husband said Captain Brehm had returned, but I've not seen him since." She dropped her arms, her face turning somber. "He also said the negotiations were a failure."

Lucy looked around the bakery, then lowered her voice. "Perhaps we can talk in your carriage?"

"Yes, of course. Let me get my bread. You're welcome to wait there if you'd like."

A few minutes later, Adelaide climbed into her carriage and sat across from Lucy. "Here, I bought us each a raspberry tart." She smiled as she handed one to Lucy.

"Thank you. I've missed these since I left." She frowned. "Oh, Adelaide, I don't know where to start. Everything was going so well. And then the Yorkers attacked, and everything changed." She dabbed at her eyes with a handkerchief.

"I don't understand. Attacked?"

Lucy spent a few minutes explaining the events that had taken place leading up to Captain Brehm's departure in between bites of her raspberry tart.

"I fear if Vermont and the crown don't reach an agreement where both are happy, I shall never be happy again either." She fidgeted in her seat as she wrung her hands. "How can I go on?" She gulped a breath before continuing. "Captain Brehm occupies my every waking thought—and my dreams too." She allowed herself a brief, sly smile.

"I saw his interest in you before you left," Adelaide said. "So it continued in Vermont?"

"It was wonderful." She brushed a stray lock of hair from her cheek. "We grew closer after he got my brother released from New York. We'd play chess—he bought me a beautiful set." Her eyes lit up. "We'd play and talk about all sorts of things. I hadn't felt anything like that since..." She cast her eyes down. "... since my husband was killed."

"I'm so sorry, Lucy." Adelaide reached out and took Lucy's hands in hers. "Is there anything I can do for you?"

Lucy took a deep breath. "I was hoping you would intercede on my behalf, on our behalf, with Captain Brehm. I have a letter." She reached into her bodice and pulled out the waiting letter. As she did so, her thumb pressed into the wax seal that had been warmed next to her bosom. She handed it to Adelaide.

Adelaide tucked the letter into her purse. "I'll send a note to my husband to invite him to dinner tonight."

"Oh, thank you!" Lucy took a deep breath as relief flooded over her.

"Where are you staying? I'll take you there."

Lucy blushed and pointed to the stone houses across the square. "Just over there."

"Well, I'm certainly glad we ran into each other—by chance," Adelaide said, flashing a knowing smile.

———— ◆◇◆ ————

Captains Brehm and Johnson were meeting with Frederick Haldimand in the governor general's house. The fortified cliff-top house—a series of conjoined, four-story stone buildings forming an *L*—was illuminated in varying hues of tan as sun and shadow danced upon them. A procession of chimneys penetrated their onyx slate roofs. An Anglican church, originally a Catholic cathedral, stood opposite one row of buildings. The ornately decorated governor's office occupied the top floor. His massive chestnut desk faced east, providing him an expansive view of the St. Lawrence River. Two dozen cannons lined against the walled fortifications, protecting the city from a naval assault.

Haldimand, sixty years old with penetrating dark eyes below thick, black eyebrows, sat behind his desk. What remained of his once black hair had long since turned stark white around his monk-like bald spot. "Excellent report, Captain," Haldimand said, giving Brehm a curt nod. "But you mention no resolution of the kidnapped New Yorkers."

"I left after the Vermonters refused to free them in exchange for their colonel I brought back from Albany," Brehm responded, frowning as he recalled his argument with Ira his last evening in Bennington. "They were going to place them on trial. Based on the vehement feelings, it was abundantly clear the outcome of any trial would be preordained. I didn't want to stay and witness that."

"Most unfortunate. When I sent you on the mission, I had high hopes for a peaceful resolution and their rejoining the empire." Brehm pursed his lips and shifted his weight.

Haldimand looked down at the report and shuffled some papers. Looking back at Brehm, he continued, "You state in your report that Mr. Allen was reasonable, but there were more radical elements of their council."

"Yes, that was my assessment. And Mr. Allen stated the same my last night there—the radicals had a slim majority."

"Your evaluation of their military capabilities is of the most immediate interest." He gazed again at the papers on his desk, picked one up, and read, "'Well trained, disciplined, fiercely loyal, and without fear. But limited manpower leaves them vulnerable to a coordinated attack from multiple fronts.'" Haldimand looked at Brehm. "Excellent work, captain. If Vermont won't return peacefully, we'll convince them on the battlefield. A spring offensive will show them the might of the crown."

"Yes, sir," Brehm replied. *What have I wrought for Vermont—and Lucy?*

"Your new knowledge of the geography of Vermont will be most useful in planning the assault. That will be all for now. You're both dismissed."

After they exited the governor's office, the governor's secretary stopped Captain Johnson. "Sir, there's a note that was delivered here for you while you were in the governor's office." He handed the sealed note to Johnson.

"Thank you, Lieutenant." He and Brehm strode out of the ante-room. "It's from Adelaide," Johnson said, "I hope there isn't an issue." He pried the seal open as they continued to walk together. He glanced over the note and stopped short.

Having taken a few extra steps, Brehm stopped and turned to his friend. "Is there a problem?"

Johnson tilted his head slightly then gave Brehm a quizzical look. "This is unusual but certainly welcome."

"What?" Brehm asked, getting exasperated at his friend's equivoca-tion.

He stared at the paper again. "Adelaide wants me to invite you to dinner this evening," he said, looking Brehm in the eye. He straight-ened his posture and formally said, "Captain Brehm, would you care to join my wife and me for dinner this evening at our residence?"

"I would be honored, Captain Johnson." Their laughter echoed off the high ceilings as they continued their way out of the governor general's house.

That evening, Brehm and Johnson sat in the latter's parlor enjoying a bottle of claret that Brehm had brought as a dinner gift. Brehm was regaling him with a colorful version of his time in Albany with the New York governor when Adelaide entered.

"Mrs. Johnson, it's a pleasure to see you again," Brehm said, stand-ing. "Thank you for the dinner invitation this evening." He gave a slight bow.

"Oh, captain," Adelaide said, with a little dismissive wave of her hand, "you know you're welcome here anytime. And besides, I haven't seen you since your return to the city. I'd like to hear more about your time in Vermont." She smiled pleasantly. "Plus, I have a gift for you." She walked over to a cherrywood end table, opened the small drawer, and retrieved Lucy's letter. "Mrs. Armistead is here."

"Lucy is here?" Brehm's eyes darted to the parlor entrance.

"Well, not here. But in the city. I saw her today. She gave me this for you." She handed the letter to Brehm.

With his hand slightly trembling, Brehm took the letter and stared at it momentarily. Haldimand's plans for a spring offensive echoed in his mind. "I think I need something stronger than this claret." Just before slipping the letter in his breast pocket, he allowed his finger to linger on the wax impression of Lucy's finger.

Johnson handed him a brandy, then poured one for himself. "Aren't you going to read it?"

Brehm sat. "I think I'd rather read it later. Privately." Turning to Adelaide, he asked, "Where? Where did you see her? Was she with anyone?"

"At Boulangerie Demange earlier today. She was alone. But she said her brother Mr. Allen was there along with some other Vermonters. They're interested in reopening negotiations but cannot get their letters to you or the governor. That's why she asked me to deliver that one to you."

Brehm looked at Johnson, frowning. "I didn't know they were here. The governor doesn't know." He rubbed his temples. "Robert, we'll need to discuss this with the governor tomorrow."

"That we will," Johnson replied. "Meanwhile, I'm getting hungry. And the smell of that food is making my mouth water." He stood up, holding his arm out. "Shall we?"

Captain Brehm rose from his seat to follow them to the dining room. As he did so, he patted Lucy's letter in his breast pocket.

Chapter 10

Rebuff

Theodore Brehm turned over once again in his bed. He'd lost count of how many times he had done so. Thoughts tumbled through his head. *The men from Albany have been returned—there are no barriers to negotiations. But there are barriers. Haldimand refuses any new talks. And I am to help plan a spring offensive.* He kicked his blanket off and flipped over again. *Damn it, Brehm. You must get some sleep.* He concentrated on his breathing. Deep breaths.

The memory of the last time he saw his father—when he was sixteen and leaving Northamptonshire—jumped to mind. *"You're an ensign now, in the service of His Majesty, with all the rights and privileges that entails. It is your duty now to support and defend the crown. Make me proud!"* It was the last time I saw him. How he would have loved Lucy.

What did Lucy write? "A way forward for Vermont and the crown." Isn't that my duty, too? How many men will it take to suppress Vermont? She'd asked. How many, indeed? Can we afford to spare the troops it will take? The damned French would want that. Anything that hurts the Empire. I shall discuss this with the governor tomorrow—no, today. Peace is in the interest of England, of the king himself.

He opened his eyes. *Am I allowing my feelings to cloud my judgment? The governor general wants Vermont to be entirely under the crown. Somehow, in some fashion, Vermont must be integrated. I must find a middle ground.* He closed his eyes and lay still. But sleep did not come. His mind jumped from Lucy and the Green Mountains to the troops they'd have to deploy. *I will convince Governor Haldimand. I must.*

———◦○◦———

"I checked and found that the Vermonters have been attempting to deliver letters for you and the governor through the magistrate," Johnson said to Brehm as they walked to the governor general's house in the morning.

"Without success, otherwise I would have received them by now." Brehm yawned, dark circles under his eyes. "I think we should let those letters come through and see what they have to say."

"I'm glad to hear you say that, as it echoed my thoughts when I learned about them. Plus, I've already sent word to the magistrate to accept the letters—if they attempt to deliver them again today—and bring them here."

"I'm surprised the Vermonters are here, and quickly too," Brehm said. "I haven't been back a week. Lucy's letter mentioned the Albany men were returned, but not why. Either they reconsidered holding a trial, or something else happened. Hopefully, these letters explain it all."

They arrived at the governor general's house, presented themselves to the young lieutenant in the anteroom outside the governor's office, and waited. Though the governor wasn't expecting them, based on his experience Brehm didn't expect to wait long. This time, though, the wait seemed unusually long.

After an hour, the office door opened, and Major General Guy Bell, the military commander in Trois-Rivières known for his ruthless tactics, stepped out. He was also the Indian agent responsible for the Mohawk and Iroquois nations' alliance with the British during the suppressed American rebellion. A tall man with fiery red hair and ice-green eyes that matched his green and red regimental, Bell strode past them in quiet determination. The lieutenant jumped up from behind his desk, grabbed some correspondence, and entered the governor's office, closing the door behind him, temporarily leaving Brehm and Johnson alone.

Johnson leaned toward Brehm. "What could General Bell possibly be here for?" he whispered

Brehm frowned and bit his lip. "I don't trust him," he said quietly. "And I never liked him," remembering the skirmish where Bell scalped six men. "His tactics are..." He paused, searching for the right word. "... harsher than required."

"I've read some of the reports." Johnson shuddered. "I can't imagine."

The office door creaked open, and the lieutenant returned. "The governor will see you now."

"Captain Brehm, Captain Johnson, I did not expect you to be back so quickly," Haldimand greeted the pair as they entered his office.

"There's been a development we think you need to be aware of," Johnson said. "A Vermont delegation arrived in the city. They're in Lower Town, but a letter from them is coming." He left out mention of the letter to Brehm.

"Hmm, interesting," Haldimand said, glancing at a letter on his desk. "Do we know what they want?"

"To reopen negotiations," Brehm said. "After my abrupt departure, they released the New Yorkers. Though we need to see the letter, I think it's worth seeing what they have to offer."

Haldimand considered the two men standing before him, looking from one to the other. "You're considerably well informed on this development." He picked up correspondence from his desk. "The lieutenant brought this in just a few minutes ago. It's the Vermonters' letter. Indeed, they do ask to continue negotiations."

Perhaps we can settle this here, Brehm thought. *Maybe all isn't lost.* "Sir, there were wide areas of agreement while I was in Bennington, as I indicated in my report." He gestured to his report, which was still on the governor's desk. "Where we disagreed was on their insistence on independence."

"No, never," Haldimand interrupted. "The crown would never accept that, and neither shall I."

"Yes, sir. That was my position throughout my time there." Brehm hesitated. *My words here may make all the difference.* "I've always had the interest of the empire as my highest priority. I've thought about this again and again. We have six thousand men at our disposal in Quebec. But almost a thousand of them are stationed at our western outposts in defense against the French."

"Yes, yes, I know all that." Haldimand waved his hand dismissively.

"This city we hold still retains French loyalists. That's been a preoccupation of ours since we took her." Lucy's voice echoed in his mind. "How many men would we need to suppress Vermont? You quoted from my report yesterday: Their rangers are well trained, disciplined, fiercely loyal, and without fear."

"You also stated they had limited manpower. What are you getting at, Captain?"

"We can defeat them. We would defeat them. But it's going to take a larger force to overwhelm them. Can we spare them all from this city? A city the French would love to occupy once again. And how large an occupying force would we need once we defeat them? We're stretched in the American colonies, having to keep on guard for the militias they were allowed to maintain. I expect we'd have to do the same in Vermont."

"And the alternative, Captain?" Haldimand asked. "Allow an insignificant little area to flaunt their independence at us? France would love that."

There it is! There's my opening. "Not flaunt. What if we reached an agreement with them? An agreement as an ally. One that is aligned with the crown's interests—and can act in concert with us against the French. We could deploy our men to shore up positions against French expansion with such an agreement."

Haldimand leaned back in his chair and considered Brehm's suggestion. "No. They had the opportunity to rejoin the empire peacefully and retain their rights as British citizens. No, we shall not allow this little republic to stand against us."

Brehm's shoulders slumped. He glanced at Johnson, his eyes pleading. "Governor, might we consider using the threat of imminent invasion as a tactic in new negotiations?" Johnson asked. "They're here—"

"No." Haldimand slammed his fist on his desk. "We plan a spring offensive. I'm drawing up a letter to General Clinton so we can use men from New York as a southern force. And I've tasked General Bell with recruiting the Mohawk and Iroquois in the fight. We'll have the manpower to overwhelm. That will be all, gentlemen. You're dismissed."

Brehm was ashen as he walked out of the office. The atmosphere was a reversal of their mood the afternoon before as they left the governor's residence. *My God, Bell's troops and Indians in Vermont! How can I allow this to happen to Lucy? I must find a way to stop this.*

"Lieutenant, get in here," Haldimand gruffly called.

"Yes, sir?"

"Send word to the magistrate that the Vermont delegation is no longer welcome in Quebec."

———— ◆ ————

Captain Johnson was home when word reached him from the governor's secretary that the Vermonters would be expelled from Quebec. The magistrate was to inform them they had twenty-four hours to leave. Adelaide overheard the message delivered to her husband, and her thoughts spiraled. *Lucy will be devastated. She can't hear it from a nameless, faceless clerk. I must let her know.*

"I'm going shopping, Robert," Adelaide said to her husband. "There's some errands I must attend to."

"Yes," he replied absently. "I need to attend to work with Captain Brehm anyway."

Her carriage pulled to the front door, and Adelaide climbed aboard.

"Where to madam?" said the driver with a tip of his hat.

"Boulangerie Demange," she replied, taking a seat.

The weather had grown pronouncedly colder, the sky accumulating ashen clouds. She pulled her woolen cloak closer to her body, her hands inside for warmth. When they reached the bakery, Adelaide exited and ordered the driver to wait down the road for her. She watched him drive off. Satisfied he was sufficiently far away, Adelaide crossed the square to the rented rooms Lucy had pointed out just the day before. Each step felt heavier as dread built within her. As she approached the door to knock, the door opened, and Lucy appeared. The genuine warmth of her smile filled Adelaide with guilt.

"I saw you walking from my window. Do you have news already from my letter?" she asked excitedly.

"Can we talk in private?" Adelaide nodded her head inside to the warmth.

"Of course."

Once inside, Adelaide removed her cloak, thankful for the warmth of the fireplace. "I gave the captain your letter last night at dinner—"

"And?"

"He was initially surprised but seemed excited. Though he didn't read it right away." Lucy looked crestfallen as Adelaide continued, "Something happened today. I haven't been able to find out what."

"Really?" Lucy leaned forward eagerly.

"Oh, Lucy, I'm so sorry to have to tell you, but I wanted to be here for you when you found out. Governor Haldimand has ordered the Vermont delegation expelled from Quebec!"

Lucy staggered backward until she felt the bed behind her knees, and collapsed on it. Adelaide sat beside her, placing comforting arms around her shoulders.

"What of Theodore?" Lucy faltered.

"I just don't know. By my husband's reaction, the news shocked him. I'm certain Captain Brehm didn't have anything to do with this. Otherwise, Robert would have known."

Lucy sat up, and Adelaide embraced her. Pulling away, Lucy asked,

"Why? For what reason?"

"I don't know." Adelaide furrowed her brow. "I'll see what other information I can find out."

"Oh, please! I need to know before we're sent away." Desperation crept into her voice.

"I will. I need to know you're going to be all right."

"I'm heartbroken." She lowered her gaze, wiping her eyes with the sleeve of her dress. "I thought... I thought Theodore would visit. I convinced myself he would." Lucy looked up. "Does Ira know yet?"

"I don't know that either." They sat together for a moment in silence. "I should go see if I can find out anything else. But only if you're going to be all right," she added.

"Yes. Go see if there's other news. Thank you, Adelaide."

The two stood up, and Adelaide embraced her again. Adelaide left the room without saying another word. Lucy stood at the window, watching Adelaide make her way across the square, before sitting at the writing desk. She dipped the quill in the inkwell, and wrote.

Captain Brehm,

I've just heard the devastating news we are to be expelled from Quebec.

Lucy held the paper and looked at the words. *What can I write? I've already poured my heart into the letter Adelaide delivered. And where did that get us? Expelled.* She crumpled up the paper and threw it in the fireplace. The flames consumed it.

———◆◆◆———

Theodore Brehm sat alone in his office, rethinking the meeting with Haldimand and his expulsion of the Vermonters. *What could I have done differently? The plan makes sense, both for the crown and Vermont.* He got up and paced the small room. Six steps, and he was at the window. The inky clouds rolled across the sky over the street drills of the 31st Regiment of Foot in their madder red regimentals and white facings, cocked hats, and knee-high spatterdashes. In his imagination, they were marching over the Green Mountains. He shook himself. *My duty. My country. My king.* He rubbed his forehead. *My love.* With the thought of Lucy, he refocused. *I must see her, speak with her before she leaves.* He sighed. *How can I? I'll make it worse on her. And if there's war and I'm sent to Vermont?* He ran his fingers through his hair, reached into his breast pocket, and pulled out her letter. He let his finger linger on her wax thumbprint, then opened it again. *Let me at least respond.* He sat at his desk and wrote.

Dearest Lucy,

My heart is heavy as I write this. I have just learned of the governor's orders for the Vermont delegation to leave Quebec. Know that I interceded on your behalf, alas, to no avail. For that, I am deeply sorry. I fear that I have failed you and must make amends for it. I will continue exploring every conceivable way to reach a just and lasting peace and work tirelessly to convince the governor. We should not be on opposing sides. The cause of the crown and the cause of Vermont are intertwined.

I long to see you and miss our conversations. I even miss how you beat me at chess. One day, and I hope soon, we will be together again. I dreamt of you and the Green Mountains the other night—

There was a knock at the door, and Captain Johnson entered. He didn't bother to greet him. "News, Theodore: The Vermonters left the city. I didn't expect it so quickly."

Brehm stared in disbelief. "How did it come to this?" His jaw tightened as he balled his fist, slamming it on the table in frustration. "There must be a way..." Brehm's voice trailed, his eyes landing on his unfinished letter as if it would answer him. He bit his lip, folded the letter into quarters, and placed it in his breast pocket.

———◆———

Ira Allen's mind spun with schemes to reopen negotiations as they rode through Lower Town. "What could we offer that we haven't?" he muttered. *Freedom of movement through Vermont? Military alliance? One thing is certain: The council will never accept total capitulation—and neither will I.* "He has no desire for negotiations," he rasped. *There must be a way to prevent war.*

"What did those letters contain that once they were delivered, we were so unceremoniously kicked out of the city?" Lucy asked, casting a wary eye to the western sky.

Ira gripped the reins tighter. "Details about the return of the Yorkers and our desire to return to the negotiating table. Praise for Captain Brehm in the one for the governor. I would have hoped the letter to the captain would have resulted in a response. I thought him an honorable man."

"We don't even know if he received his letter," Lucy responded. "Maybe he didn't have a chance to respond or intercede with the governor. Everything happened so quickly today."

"The governor received the correspondence," Ira said, his face buffeted by the cold breeze. "I would believe Captain Brehm did as well."

Lucy didn't respond. Her mind was on Brehm. *Was that really the last time I'll ever see him? His back as he rode off in Bennington.* She flipped up the hood of her red wool cloak so Ira couldn't see her tears forming. The snow began to fall.

Chapter 11

No Promises

Baron von Steuben and Pierre du Ponceau walked the grounds of von Steuben's headquarters camp, the baron leaning on his carved hickory cane. He still walked with a noticeable limp and likely would for the rest of his life. Azor accompanied him—that is, when he wasn't running off to sniff something interesting.

"*Gottverdammt!*" the baron cursed as his cane sank into a soft patch of earth, almost causing him to fall.

"You really need to learn to speak English," Pierre said. "I know you can. You understand it well enough."

"Why?" asked the baron. "I have you with me."

"I may not always be around."

"Pfft. Where are you going?"

Pierre shrugged. "I have no firm plans. But what if it were I who was shot instead of you? Where would that have left you?" They stopped to allow the baron to rest his leg. "Vermont needs you, especially now. You speaking English would make planning easier."

"General Warner doesn't mind." The baron waved off Pierre's suggestions with his free hand. "I've seen you two have conversations on strategy as well."

"I'm not the inspector general of the republic's army. It would behoove you to speak their language. Our language now."

"No promises," the baron said as he started his walk again.

"Mr. Allen's delegation to Quebec, if they fail in reopening negotiations—"

"We need to be prepared for battle," interrupted the baron.
"Though I don't anticipate they'll attempt a winter invasion. No
one would be that rash." He smirked at Pierre, knowing they were
both thinking about John Hancock's disastrous decision the previous
winter to attack the British base at Newport, Rhode Island, leading
directly to the defeat of the Northern Continental Army. Of course,
their dismissal before that battle led to their settling in Vermont.

"Either way, plans are in place. The key is manpower, for while I
am confident of our ability on the battlefield, we alone cannot hope
to match the British in troops." He grimaced, then whistled. Azor
came running from the forest. His leg throbbed, a stark reminder of
his limitations. "Back to camp," he muttered, frustration creeping into
his voice.

———•◦•———

Governor Haldimand sat behind his desk, the midmorning sunlight
providing ample light for his work. He had just received a dispatch of
correspondence and was sorting through the letters, prioritizing them.
When he came across the folded letter, closed with Lord North's wax
seal, he opened it immediately.

Letter from Lord North, Prime Minister of Great
Britain:

Whitehall, 8th October 1778

His Excellency Governor Haldimand,
Since I last wrote to you, news from our operatives in
Paris has reached me. They report that the French have
an interest in reigniting rebellion in our North American colonies as a precursor to retaking the province
of Quebec. A marquis recently returned from North
America has been agitating within King Louis XVI's
inner circle and may have had some influence to this effect. The Parliament of Great Britain is perfectly united
in opinion and determined to pursue the most effectual
measures and to use the whole force of the Kingdom, if
it be found necessary, to maintain and hold the province
of Quebec and to suppress any rebellious French resi-
dents.

The defense of our North American colonies and
provinces is of the utmost importance. Such being the
case, it is judged necessary that British troops be in a
state of readiness to act against French incursions upon
our lands. The exception being already made by Parliament itself of the necessity of guarding against disaf-
fected persons in the colonies where the peace agreement has been so justly instituted.

You will naturally make a proper use of troops to defend the Province of Quebec from French expeditions. Parliament has authorized payment of 8000 pounds sterling for supplies of provisions for British troops in Canada to maintain our outposts, fortifications, and towns. You are to inform me of your plans, troop numbers, and deployment.

I have the honour to be, with great respect, Sir, Your most obedient and humble servant.
Right Honorable Lord North

He read through it a second time. *No mention of Vermont. I informed the prime minister of Captain Brehm's mission, yet he neglected to mention it here. The proper use of troops to defend Quebec! What does he think I'm doing? We have a rebellious colony to our south! I'll inform him of our plans to take Vermont for the crown. But I won't risk receiving a countermanding order. The invasion must move up. We will crush this rebellious colony and return them to the crown.*

———◆———

General Guy Bell was back at the governor's residence. Along with him were Captains Brehm and Johnson. They stood on either side of an immense walnut table in the ornately decorated green room. Elaborately carved crown molding framed the vivid turquoise patterned wallpaper, which gave the room its name, rising above the ivory-painted chair rail along the room's perimeter. Landscape paintings peppered the walls, and a crackling fire burned in the large fireplace opposite the windows. Governor Haldimand had rolled out a map of New York, Quebec, and New England on the table. The men hunched over, examining it.

The major settlements of Vermont were marked, along with other known fortifications. While the Green Mountains would be a formidable range to travel over in a winter campaign, it would also prevent east and west Vermont from quickly moving troops in defense against attacks.

"If we launch from Montreal by the end of November, we'll still be able to use Lake Champlain," Bell said, tracing his finger on the map down the lake. "Our Mohawk allies travel with us. South of Fort Ticonderoga, we head overland. The Abenaki Indians are on friendly terms with the Mohawk, and I expect no issues with passing by their settlements." He stood upright and directed his gaze at Brehm, his mouth transforming into a menacing smile. "The Mohawk are excellent at spreading fear among the settlers with war cries." Brehm clenched his fists, hidden from view below the table.

Bell continued, "Surprise is the key. We take the first town at night while they sleep. By the time the sun rises, we have the town leaders in irons and order everyone else to stay in their homes on pain of being shot if they come out." Haldimand gazed at Bell unblinking and in rapt attention as Bell carried on. "By the time we reach Bennington, news of our campaign will have preceded us. Intimidation and the threat of violence should suffice. If not, we unleash our allies."

"And if the snows come early again as they did last year, what then?" Brehm asked, keeping his voice level, though he felt as if Haldimand could hear his heart pounding. "Your men could be stranded." Brehm turned to speak directly to the governor. "Should we risk an expedition to the vagaries of the weather? Aren't we better off launching an attack in the spring?" *I need to find a way to delay this. Maybe diplomacy can succeed in the meantime. I can't allow Bell's savage force to destroy Vermont.*

"Time is of the essence, Captain," Haldimand replied. "We must demonstrate that the British Empire will not tolerate more rebellions." He leaned back over the map. "Captain, you traveled the Connecticut River on your way to Bennington. We'll be able to travel overland following the river's course until it's navigable." He traced his finger down the river and looked up at Brehm. "The first town of any stature is Windsor, here." He tapped the map at Windsor, about 300 miles south of Quebec. "Mostly civilian, as you noted in your report, but there was a detachment of their Green Mountain Rangers from among the local population. You said this Prussian general—what was his name?"

"General von Steuben, sir."

"Ah yes, a baron, I believe? You said he has forged these rangers into a formidable fighting force."

"Yes, sir." *Perhaps stressing their fierceness and efficiency will deter this expedition.* "They made quick work of the New Yorkers when they attacked before I left."

"Militia," Bell interjected. "Mostly left over from the rebellion. They weren't fearsome then; they aren't now."

"Still, the rangers suffered no casualties—except von Steuben's leg wound," Brehm said, switching again to their efficiency on the battlefield. "While the New Yorkers suffered a number, and the rest of them scurried back across the border."

"I think a force of several hundred well-trained and equipped British soldiers will make quick work of Windsor," Haldimand said. His attention returned to the map. "And from there, on to Brattleboro. Smaller than Windsor and the only other town of any consequence in the colony. Once we control these three towns, they will have no option but to capitulate."

"The threat of violence will keep them in line," Bell said. "Once they're subdued, we offer a promise of non-interference with their local governments. They can continue about their business—but as subjects of the king."

"Captain Johnson," Haldimand directed his unblinking eyes at him. "I want you and Captain Brehm to prepare a plan that includes recommended force size, supplies, and route. I want that plan to me in two days' time. That will be all, Captains. You're dismissed."

They saluted and left, leaving the governor conferring with General Bell.

Lucy shivered under her wool blanket. She didn't know what had woken her: the wolves howling nearby or her dream about Theodore. *I could hear his voice clearly and smell his scent. Why wouldn't he see me?* She buried her face in her bedroll, trying to push away the lingering dream. A wolf howled again, and she wrapped the blanket tighter. Sleep came fitfully.

She rose before dawn, restarting the fire and boiling water. Some she used for the tea she had carried from Quebec City; the rest she poured into the remains of the previous night's stew for breakfast.

They'd been traveling for a week, paralleling the Connecticut River south. Their rations were meager, supplemented by whatever rabbits and squirrels they could catch and kill. Ira joined her by the fire, and she handed him a cup of tea.

"You had a restless night, I fear," he said, his hands in fingerless gloves wrapped around the mug for warmth.

"The wolves," Lucy answered.

"And dreams. I heard you utter 'Theodore.'" He looked at her, then reached out and touched the back of her hand.

Lucy looked away from his gaze and at the fire, listening to the log sizzle and crackle. "I did dream of him. I thought he would have come to see us. See me. Though Adelaide said she hadn't seen him since his return."

"Adelaide?" Ira asked, his voice incredulous. "You spoke with Mrs. Johnson?"

Lucy sighed. "I did. I saw her the day before we were told to leave. She said she would tell Captain Brehm we were there. Oh, Ira, I was so hopeful that night. Then nothing. No message, no visit." She blew on her fingers, then spread her hands in front of the fire, watching the flames dance. "I don't think he has any feelings for me."

Ira considered her for a moment. "No. I don't think that's it." He stayed silent until Lucy looked at him in anticipation. "He's a British officer. What would happen if he was reported meeting with us—you—without approval?" He shook his head. "Lucy, I saw how he looked at you, how his countenance changed when he was with you." He frowned. "But he has his duty. I can only hope he has some influence with the governor." *Because I've failed Vermont.*

"If there's a war—" she started, then bit her lip to keep from saying it out loud. *If there's a war, he may be leading the fighting. Then where does that leave me, us? Enemies.* Images of fallen men littering a field and homes ablaze sprang to mind.

The other delegation members wandered over to the fire from their tents. Lucy caught her brother's eye and conveyed her silent thoughts in that glance. She then busied herself to make more tea for the rest of the traveling party.

———◄O►———

Brehm sat on the edge of his bed in his linen nightshirt, his gaze landing on the letter from Lucy on the nightstand. He reached out for it and stared at her script in the candlelight. Turning the letter over, he brushed his fingers over the wax impression of her thumbprint, longing to cradle her hands in his. *I should have visited her. I shouldn't have let her go without telling her how I feel.* He imagined her eyes sparkling with green and gold. His hands trembled as he opened the letter and reread it, hearing her voice in his mind. *I'm sorry, Lucy. I'm trying to find a way to avoid war. Robert thinks it's foolish as well, especially now. He's heard through sources that the French have designs on retaking Quebec.*

Brehm refolded Lucy's letter, placed it back on his nightstand, and walked to the window, gazing at the quarter moon. *I wonder if Lucy is looking at the moon right now.* Sighing heavily, he paced the room, hoping a resolution would come to him. On his desk, he spotted the report he and Robert had prepared for their meeting with the governor the following day. *As much as I want otherwise, I have my duty.* Picking it up, he scanned the details again. *Our report is thorough, but it will require more men than the governor thinks it will if we're to hold those towns.* "Damn him," Brehm cursed aloud. *Robert and I agree the capture of Vermont should be coordinated with troops from the south. If I recommend that—and the governor approves—it could stave off the expedition at least until spring. On the other hand, when we attack, Vermont will be destroyed.*

He gnashed his teeth and tossed the plan back on his desk. Snuffing out the lantern, he laid down, expecting another restless night.

———◦———

Two weeks after leaving Quebec City, the delegation arrived in Windsor, where they intended to resupply before continuing their journey to Bennington. Windsor lay along the banks of the Connecticut River, nestled in a relatively flat plain surrounded by mountains. It was along one path that the British could take if they invaded.

Ira led them to the Windsor Tavern, where the year before he had signed the Vermont Constitution. The two-story white clapboard building with a full-length porch and green shutters was the gathering place for all important business. There, they were greeted by the proprietor, Elijah West. West was known for his barrel chest, rough hands, and long black beard streaked with gray.

Ira learned that West was now the captain of the local Green Mountain Rangers. While West gathered some of his rangers, the travelers warmed themselves by the brick fireplace. They ordered meals of meat and vegetable pies: pork combined with onions, potatoes, carrots, and parsnips.

Once West returned with half a dozen men, Ira briefed them on his mission and explained the precarious position Vermont was in. His instructions were clear: if a British force was spotted heading south, either by river or land, they were to send word to Bennington so that a viable defense could be set up. They were also to delay them if possible, but not at the risk of the destruction of the town.

The group spent the night in rooms at the tavern before resupplying provisions and traveling to their next destination, Brattleboro, by a hired flat-bottomed pink. They were in Brattleboro in three days' time.

———◦———

"Your plan dovetails nicely with General Bell's plans for a western attack," Haldimand said to Captains Brehm and Johnson, seated across from him in his office. Heat radiated from the fireplace behind him, the log in the fireplace popping as the flames licked the wood. "Your concerns about logistics and supplies are noted. The expedition shall be suitably provisioned." He flipped to another page of their report. "The troop strength you recommend is double my expectation, though."

"Well, sir," Brehm ventured, "we could reduce that in half—if our forces in New York concurrently attacked from the south. We wouldn't be burdened with maintaining control in Windsor and then moving on Brattleboro."

"Establishing that coordination would delay our plans." Haldimand's voice rose. "That's not acceptable."

Brehm hesitated, then countered in a steady voice. "Would we not be better off ensuring we have the proper forces to overwhelm them?"

"Captain," Haldimand stared at Brehm, who straightened in his seat. "I appreciate your recommendations, but you and Captain Johnson have laid out a detailed plan. I intend to review this with General Bell."

A rap on his office door and the sudden appearance of his secretary interrupted Haldimand. "Excuse me, sir. But a letter just arrived on a frigate. It came with a note from the ship's captain stating that he was handed the letter personally by General Clinton, who asked that no delay be made in delivering it to you upon its arrival."

"Bring it here," Haldimand said, motioning with an outstretched arm.

Letter from General Henry Clinton, Commander of New York:

N. York, 1st November 1778

Sir,
The Intelligence for which I have some days detained the Frigate is at length arrived—

My agents are returned from Albany and our Indian allies. Reports brought by my Agents from good Authority respecting the French having laid aside their Intention against N York, instead intend upon Quebec and to support Vermont in action against the crown. The Enemy troops prepare in the Course of the Winter, to make Preparation for a more Effectual Essay in the Spring.

How far Encroachments by the enemy in Quebec may encourage the French populace to Rebellion is of concern. Fearing on the one side that sending troops from N. York to aid Quebec will weaken our ability to de-

fend against Vermont and French forces acting in concert—but in so Critical a Juncture I most sensibly feel
the want of specific Instructions. My loyalty to the
King's service guides my actions and therefore I see
with much Concern that our troop strength needs to
be maintained for the defense of N. York—at least as
things are at present circumstanced.

Your Excellency will understand my decision absent any
contravening orders. Our preparations this Winter for
potential expedition against the enemy come Spring
will, if carried on expeditiously, I should hope prove
Successful.

I have the Honour & etc.
His Excy. General Sir H. Clinton

Haldimand's cheeks flushed as he read the letter silently. "Did you
have foreknowledge of this letter, Captain?" He rose, jabbing the letter
at Brehm.

The two captains leaped to their feet. "I'm sorry, sir?" Brehm stammered. "I don't understand."

"This letter from General Clinton." Haldimand waved the correspondence in his clenched fist. "He says his troops are needed in
New York." He turned his back to the men and strode to the window,
looking over the likely last ships to dock before the St. Lawrence froze.

Despite the warmth of the fire, Brehm felt a chill as he watched
Haldimand's back at the frosted window. Haldimand turned and

shouted, "Out," pointing to the door. "I shall send for you when I want you."

Brehm and Johnson exchanged worried glances as they left the office. *My God,* thought Brehm, *he could launch the attack earlier. And with my plan.* He swallowed hard, his thoughts turning to Lucy.

Chapter 12

Second Thoughts

The delegation's trip back from Quebec City took a week longer than their two-week trip north. They arrived in Bennington after sundown, exhausted, muddy, cold, and hungry. A freak morning snowstorm the day before, which quickly melted in the afternoon sun, left them slogging through ankle-deep mud.

Ira and Lucy split off from the others and headed straight for Ira's home. Lucy started a fire in the fireplace, washed up in cold well water, and changed into clean clothing. The two were about to walk to the tavern for a meal when their brother Ethan arrived carrying a clay pot of stew and a wooden bucket full of ale.

"I thought you might be hungry," Ethan said with a huge smile. He placed the pot and bucket on the long table against the wall.

"Ethan!" Lucy and Ira moved to give him a hug.

"Let's get a lantern lit in here. I can't see much by that firelight." He fetched a lantern hanging on a wall hook by the dining table. "I saw the others straggle into the tavern," he said while lighting the candles. "It sure looked like you had some rough travels."

Ira stood by the fireplace, warming himself. "Ethan…" Ira cast his eyes down, his mouth opening as if to speak again, but no words came. His shoulders slumped under the weight of the failed diplomatic mission. The only sound in the room was the crackling fire. Finally, he looked at his brother, his voice dry. "We failed, Ethan. I think this means war."

Lucy's eyes darted between her brothers. Her stomach tightened as she watched Ethan's reaction. Ethan crossed the room to Ira's side and guided him to a chair. "Come now, have a drink, let's talk." He turned to his sister, still standing. "Lucy, you too." He scooped a mug of ale out of the pail for each of them. "Let's start from the beginning."

Ira detailed their time in Quebec City, with Lucy interjecting additional details and mentioning her, as she called it, fortuitous meeting with Adelaide. Ira also told of their stopping in Windsor and Brattleboro and their meeting with town leaders.

When they were done relating their experiences, Ethan sat back and stroked the stubble on his chin, looking between his siblings. "Then I agree," he said, pursing his lips. "We must prepare for war." He stood up, placing a hand on Ira's shoulder. "Get some rest. We'll meet with General Warner and the baron tomorrow." He glanced back at them as he closed the door.

———◆———

When Brehm entered Haldimand's office a week later, the governor was standing where he last saw him—at the window gazing at the river. A small fire burned in the fireplace, leaving the room dry but still chilly. Brehm stood rigidly, waiting to be addressed.

"The river will soon be frozen over," Haldimand said without turning around. "Another winter is upon us." He continued to gaze out the window for another few minutes before speaking again, his back still to Brehm. "I have a mission for you." He turned around and gestured to the chair opposite his desk. "Sit down, Captain. I have some questions for you."

Brehm sat down, his forehead breaking into a sweat despite the room's coolness.

"Vermont." He picked up a piece of correspondence from his desk and scanned it. "Vermont still perplexes me." His dark eyes bore into Brehm. "You're the officer with the most intimate knowledge of Vermont."

Brehm flinched at Haldimand's choice of the word 'intimate,' thinking involuntarily of Lucy.

"I've received intelligence from several sources that impact my plans for Vermont."

Brehm's stomach churned.

"Impact how, sir?"

"We need Vermont aligned with the crown, one way or another. And I mean to have that completed before spring." Haldimand watched for Brehm's reaction, but Brehm held his face rigid. "You made some recommendations a few weeks ago, which have proved to be prescient, from which I've concluded you're the best man for this mission."

"Sir? A mission to Vermont?"

Haldimand slowly nodded. "The intelligence of which I spoke: The French are reportedly interested in striking an alliance with Vermont—and striking a blow at Quebec. They plan on inciting an uprising among the French populace, attacking us, and retaking the province."

"We must stop them."

"We must stop an alliance between Vermont and France if it isn't already too late." Haldimand stood and walked to the bookshelf, removing a rolled map. He spread it on his desk. Running a finger over western Quebec, he continued. "I've ordered General Bell to reinforce our outposts. I'm providing him additional men and provisions. General Clinton," he pointed at New York, "is preparing in case of French encroachment from the west and can spare no men to join us." Haldimand glanced at Brehm. "This leaves us more vulnerable to a French-Vermont alliance. This is where your mission comes in."

"Of course, sir."

"I want you to return to Bennington and strike a deal with them, but it has to be on our terms. They must join an alliance with the empire—a military alliance. A mutual defense agreement if you find that necessary. They can keep their precious republic if they agree to all our terms. We have them surrounded anyway. Without our friendship and cooperation, we'd allow no commerce, and they'd starve."

Almost my plan I presented weeks ago, thought Brehm. *Don't show your excitement, Brehm.* "I can conclude these negotiations and get them to agree."

"I thought you'd want a second chance at this."

"Yes, sir. When do you want me to leave?"

"Immediately. There's a frigate that is headed to New York tomorrow. Likely the last out before the river freezes over. I want you on it. From New York, you can travel overland to Bennington. Captain Johnson will join you on this mission. The two of you have proved to be a good team."

"Yes, sir. Thank you, sir."

"You had better prepare for your travels. You're dismissed."

Brehm saluted Haldimand, turned, and strode out of his office, and forced himself not to smile.

New York Harbor was almost empty of commercial ships. These had left the rougher and more dangerous North Atlantic winter for more profitable trade routes of sugar, rum, molasses, tobacco, rice, and indigo between the Caribbean and Europe. While a few Royal Navy vessels dotted the almost desolate docks, most of these had already sailed as well, for warmer naval bases in Charleston, Jamaica, and Antigua.

Brehm and Johnson stood on the frigate's deck and watched the buildings grow closer. A cold mist pelted them as they held the rails to avoid losing their footing on the slippery deck. Brehm wore a charcoal-gray wool greatcoat over his regimental with the collar turned up to keep his neck dry. Johnson favored a well-worn blanket capote he'd obtained in western Quebec. It was a parchment-colored natural wool coat that reached to his knees and tied tight with a cinnamon-colored leather belt. He had the hood flipped over his hat, guarding against the mist.

"You couldn't convince Mrs. Johnson to come out of her cabin?" Brehm asked, winking at Johnson, knowing full well that she disliked seeing the up-down motion of the ship against the land and houses.

"You're a devil," Johnson said in mock anger, the corners of his mouth curving up. "She'll be much happier once we disembark to dry land." He looked up at the mist striking them. "Well, land, anyway."

"I must confess, when you showed up at the dock in Quebec with your wife and enough luggage to fill the hull, I was surprised."

"Really now, it's not like three chests will change the ship's ballast. Anyway, she insisted she needed everything," Johnson said with a shrug.

Brehm laughed with his friend. "Unfortunately for Mrs. Johnson, once we dock, I plan to secure passage for us up the Hudson River to Albany. From there, we'll head to Bennington. What kind of reception we receive, we'll see." *And I'll see what kind of reception Lucy gives me after I didn't speak with her in Quebec.*

Brehm stared at the passing dock buildings—two- and three-story high wood buildings in earthy pigments of ochre, smoke, and slate crowded behind the docks. Their gambrel and gabled roofs were dotted with chimneys. Most had large doors with hoists and pulleys anchored in the upper floors for loading and unloading goods from the ships. The now mostly empty wharves of heavy timber jutted into the river, blackened from tar and age.

Johnson broke the silence. "They did travel to Quebec to reopen negotiations. There's no reason to believe they've had a change of heart."

"Hopefully not. And, Governor Haldimand entrusted me with his seal matrix." He patted his pocket. The rectangular brass seal matrix had the coat of arms for the governor general that would authenticate any signed agreements.

——◦——

A week after setting out from New York on a two-masted sloop, *Persephone* Brehm and the Johnsons arrived in Albany late morning. The sparsely booked ship allowed them more freedom to talk and the opportunity to get to know the crew. The vessel's first mate recommended staying at the Black Horse Inn, just a ten-minute walk from the docks. The crisp air and clouded sky held the threat of snow as they headed to the inn, a two-story brick-and-stone building. They rented two rooms for the night.

It also featured a tavern where they could get a hot meal. They dined there for an early afternoon meal. The Johnsons requested roast beef, served with bread and cheese. Brehm ordered the stewed oysters served with johnnycakes, a native cornmeal flatbread. The barmaid delivered the rich, cream-buttery dish in an earthenware bowl. The oysters were lightly simmered to keep them from toughening and flavored with pepper, onion, and nutmeg.

"I'm going to see Governor Jay when we're done here," Brehm said. "I've sent word ahead telling him to expect me." He speared an oyster from his bowl of stew. "The New Yorkers previously held by Vermont should have returned. I'd like to hear from the governor about his reaction and ensure they have no plans for retaliatory attacks."

"That's the last thing we need to happen while we're there," Johnson said.

"How far is it to Bennington?" Adelaide inquired.

Brehm dipped a johnnycake into the broth. "Two days by coach. Three if the roads are bad. We'll start out at sunrise tomorrow." He took a bite. "I'm eager to get there."

"For good reason, I'm sure." Adelaide grinned.

"Adelaide!" her husband scolded.

"Well, I look forward to seeing this quaint town of which you've spoken," Adelaide continued, ignoring her husband. "And seeing Mrs. Armistead in her natural environment."

"My duty is to the crown, Mrs. Johnson," Brehm said, sitting up straighter. "Of that, you can be assured."

"I'm not suggesting otherwise, Captain Brehm. Only that your..."

She peered around the room to see who might be listening. "Your travels also provide certain opportunities."

"My personal predilections, as far as they go, are secondary to securing an agreement."

"And helpful as well."

"Adelaide! That's enough." Changing the subject, Johnson said, "Do you want me to go to the governor's office with you?"

"Thank you, but that won't be necessary. I think you may have enough to deal with this afternoon." Brehm nodded toward Adelaide.

After lunch, Brehm walked to the Stadt Huys, where the governor maintained his office. Open fields and trees surrounded the three-story brick building with a steep roof and belfry. Brehm's note to the governor had been received, and he was ushered into the office upon his arrival. With the governor was his attorney general, Egbert Benson.

Brehm shook Jay's hand. "Governor, it's a pleasure to see you again under better circumstances."

"It certainly is," Jay said. "This is my Attorney General, Egbert Benson. Mr. Benson, Captain Brehm of His Majesty's forces." They shook hands. "Please, have a seat."

"Firstly, I want to ensure that the... recent troubles have concluded. And that there won't be any additional issues."

Jay eyed Brehm. "It's been made clear that we are to maintain peace. And that we have done."

"Rest assured, I shall be delivering the same message to the Vermont Council. There is to be no fighting. We will not tolerate it."

Jay nodded, his expression undecipherable.

"Second, I wanted to make sure your men returned from their, shall we say, forced stay in Vermont."

"Our men returned. Though not before being tried and found innocent."

So, they did hold a trial, Brehm thought, holding his gaze steady. "I left Bennington for consultations in Quebec prior to that."

"Our repatriated men did report they were well defended by Mr. Ethan Allen."

A spark of surprise crossed Brehm's face that Jay didn't miss.

"You know the man?" Jay asked.

"I do. He was released from British detention in early summer. I'm relieved to hear the trial ended well."

"As am I," Jay replied. "Where are you staying?"

"The Black Horse Inn. It was recommended." *Best to avoid any mention of my traveling party.*

"Will you be staying long?"

"Not at all. I'm leaving tomorrow morning."

"Please do let me know if I can be of any further assistance, Captain." Jay rose from his chair.

Brehm rose as well. "Governor." He nodded. "Mr. Benson, it was a pleasure meeting you. He stepped out of the office.

<hr>

After supper that evening, the innkeeper delivered a note to Brehm's room and stated it was left on his counter. However, he had not seen who delivered it. Brehm opened it.

> Captain Brehm,
> I have important information that you will find perti-

nent. I cannot meet you at the inn. Meet me behind the
inn at 11 o'clock this evening. It is vital no one knows
of our meeting.

Your servant.

*There is no signature. Who could this be? I don't like this. Someone
may mean us harm. But what if there is information I need?*

Just prior to the appointed time, Brehm loaded his flintlock pistol,
keeping it at his side. He stepped out of the inn, allowed his eyes to adjust to the darkness, and secreted his way around the building. Clouds
obscured the moonlight, and the night chill sent a shiver through
Brehm. There, next to the well, a shadow moved. Brehm gripped his
pistol, sweat forming on his brow despite the cold.

"I wasn't sure you'd meet me," the shadow said, stepping forward.

"Mr. Benson," Brehm whispered, his grip tightening on his pistol.
"Why the clandestine meeting?"

"There is mischief afoot of which you need to be aware. Have you
heard the French are making an alliance with Vermont? And have
designs on your province of Quebec?"

I will not confirm this; he's seeking information from me. "Tell me
more," Brehm said.

"It's a lie. A lie generated from the mind of Governor Jay."

"But why?" Brehm scoffed.

"To scuttle any agreement between the crown and Vermont. If you
thought the French were assisting Vermont, you would likely move
against them."

Unease crept up Brehm's spine. "Why tell me? What's in it for you?"

"I want peace," Benson said. "We've already been through so much."

I don't trust him. "Tell no one what you've told me," Brehm commanded.

Benson gave a curt nod and disappeared back into the shadows.

Brehm returned to the tavern, pausing at the entrance to scan the remaining patrons. Seeing nothing awry, he took a seat with his back to a wall, and ordered an ale. *Governor Haldimand's terms are predicated upon the French threat. Yet if there is no threat, the entire reason for negotiations is invalid.* He took a long draft of his ale. *The governor could move forward with his attack plans. The French will not interfere. No! I cannot allow that to occur. And what if Benson is lying? Can I be certain either way? We can achieve an agreement with Vermont. I have it within my power to secure a just peace. I will not let harm come to Lucy or the people she loves.*

———— •◦• ————

Brehm watched the bare maple trees out the carriage window on the way to Bennington. The frozen road was easier to travel than mud, though the hardened ruts made for a bone-jarring ride. Brehm sat next to Johnson. Across sat Adelaide, next to a portly businessman who illuminated them on the excruciating details of his import business. When he wasn't discussing his business, he inquired about theirs, to which they politely responded with meaningless answers, or slept. He snored loudly.

With each mile that passed, Brehm's pulse quickened. The prospect of seeing Lucy again, combined with the pressure he felt to secure an agreement, made him anxious. His conversation with Benson kept replaying in his mind.

"You're quieter than normal," Johnson whispered to Brehm while the businessman snored.

"Just going over everything in my mind," Brehm said, continuing to gaze out the window. He pulled out his pocket watch and noted the time, half past three. "The coachman said we'd get there today, though we still have another stage stop and change of horses. So it'll probably be dark. I remember this area from my return from Albany last time. We still have a way to go."

"Theodore, you're pale," Johnson said softly.

"It's nothing; I'm fine."

Johnson narrowed his gaze. "Are you sure?"

"I didn't sleep well, that's all." Brehm sighed. "There'll be rooms and dinner at the Dewey Inn. I'll be fine. But I'm sure our unexpected arrival is going to cause a stir. My priority is speaking with Mr. Ira Allen and his brother Ethan." *And hopefully, find out from them how Lucy is doing.* He glanced over at the snoring businessman before continuing. "Once we've spoken with them, I hope we can arrange to speak with the entire council."

The carriage hit a particularly deep hole and shuddered violently, waking the businessman, who immediately began talking again. As the businessman droned on, Brehm turned again to look out the window, and for a fleeting moment, he saw Lucy's face take shape in the clouds.

———◦———

Lucy sat in Ira's parlor mending a shirt by lantern light, a fire sizzling in the fireplace. Ira sat across from her, reading a copy of the *Vermont Gazette*. Lucy placed the shirt on her lap. "It's time, Ira," she said. "I need to move back to my own home."

Ira lowered the gazette peering over his round reading spectacles. "Are you sure? You know you're welcome to stay here with me."

"Yes, I'm sure. I need to move on with my life. While I was haunted by the memories in that house for so long, I think that's in the past. I've learned through all the pain that I can be happy again." She looked down at her hands as she played with a loose thread on the shirt. "Even if it's not with... " She let her voice trail off. She sat staring at the floor for a moment.

Ira crossed the few steps between them, leaned over, and hugged her. "Whatever you need, Lucy. And you know Ethan and I will be there for you."

She tried to say "I know," but the words caught in her throat. Instead, she silently nodded.

Ira returned to his seat and pretended to read the gazette while she regained her composure. "Staying here with you—and our travels—allowed me to heal," she finally said. "I think it's time for me to move on."

He looked up. "When?"

She inhaled deeply. "Tomorrow. I can load the cart with my few items here and have Old Gray pull it to my place."

"I'll help you."

"No. I'll be fine. There's not much, and you said the council will be meeting with the baron and General Warner tomorrow."

"I'll come over after the meeting then, and I can walk Old Gray back here," Ira said.

"Thank you." Lucy picked up the shirt and found her needle to continue her mending.

———◆◇◆———

This stagecoach ride is interminable, Brehm thought. *And I cannot rid myself of this nausea.* He closed his eyes and breathed deeply, rubbing his temple.

Adelaide eyed him and exchanged worried glances with her husband. The stagecoach jostled into another rut, but this time something felt different. "Whoa!" yelled the coachman, and the coach stopped, listing a bit.

"What's this all about?" fretted the businessman, having been awakened from his sleep. No one answered him. Johnson was out the door as soon as they came to a stop.

"The wheel is cracked, and we're missing several spokes," Johnson said to the coachman as he came around the side.

A quick glance and he assessed the issue. "Better get the tools." Retrieving a case from under his seat, he returned, placing the case by the broken wheel.

The others exited as the coachman pulled several items from his case: a hammer, leather straps, wooden spikes, nails.

"How can I help?" Johnson asked.

"To start, we'll have to get this wheel off to see if it's repairable." The coachman looked at the luggage tied to the back and sighed. "And to do so, we'll need to lighten the load first. Let's get started."

Brehm stepped over to assist, but a wave of nausea washed over him. He leaned against the coach and closed his eyes to steady himself. Johnson came to his side and spoke quietly with him, then guided him a few steps into the woods. Adelaide eyed her husband, who slightly shook his head.

Johnson and the coachman worked together removing the passengers' luggage and storing it on the side of the road as the businessman watched. Adelaide fretted, having lost sight of Brehm in the thick woods.

The coachman examined the nearby trees and branches. Selecting a straight oak branch for use as a lever, he chopped it off and removed the side branches. After the coachman placed a wooden block beneath the coach's frame as a fulcrum, he and Johnson used the newly fashioned lever to lift the coach a few inches so that he could remove the broken wheel and set about making repairs.

Brehm returned as the wheel was removed and sat off to the side on a log. Adelaide began to fuss over him, but he waved her off. "I'll be fine." *I cannot fall ill*, he thought. *There's much to be done. And I must make amends to Lucy.*

The repairs took several hours. Brehm's only movement was his shivering from fever. His head pounded with each strike of the coachman's hammer. When the makeshift repairs were finally complete, the sun was sinking behind the trees, the entire afternoon lost to their misfortune. The coachman lit the carriage lamps with obvious concern about traveling these roads in darkness. The journey was slow over the darkened road, and they pulled up to their stage stop hours later than intended. They would need to spend the night at the small inn, and the coachman would need to make arrangements the next day to get the wheel replaced, for the repairs would not last through to Bennington.

As they entered the inn, the smell of cooking food caused Brehm's stomach to churn. He insisted on heading to sleep immediately, claiming he was not hungry. Adelaide and her husband spoke in hushed voices throughout dinner, their concern rising as the evening wore on.

After dinner, Johnson checked in on Brehm. Sweat soaked his clothes, and his forehead was consumed by heat. "You don't look well, Theodore."

"Robert, I can't seem to shake this sickish feeling. Perhaps I have bad humors. I've been this way since we dined at the last stage stop."

"Do you think you can get some sleep?"

"I'm so tired, and I need to. But sleep has come fitfully."

"I can stay with you if you'd like."

"No, you better get back to Adelaide. Please don't tell her how ill I feel. I don't want to worry her." He managed a small smile.

"Get some rest. I'll be back early tomorrow." Johnson stepped through the doorway, then turned. "Hopefully the wheelwright will have us on our way quickly, and we can get you to Dr. Fay in Bennington." He left without waiting for an answer.

Brehm wasn't the only one to sleep fitfully. Sleep eluded Johnson as well. Whenever he closed his eyes, he thought of Brehm—lying ill by himself, refusing to admit how sick he was. Before sunrise, Johnson was out to check on him. He found Brehm sitting on the edge of the bed, still pale but with no fever.

"I hope you feel better than you look," Johnson said.

"I'm tired. But the nausea is gone, and I no longer feel like I'm burning up."

"I'm relieved to hear it. Do you feel well enough to have something to eat?"

"Perhaps some small beer. And maybe some eggs and bread." He stood up and immediately sat back down, his head swimming.

"Here, let me help you," Johnson said, moving next to him. With Johnson's assistance, Brehm was soon in the small inn tavern drinking.

Johnson went to speak with the coachman.

Adelaide stepped to the table. "Captain Brehm, I hope you feel better than you look."

Brehm managed a laugh. "Now you sound like your husband." He motioned for her to sit. "I think I'll survive." He shook his head. "For a while there, I wasn't quite sure."

Johnson returned and sat with them. "The coachman tells me we won't be on our way again until this afternoon. Apparently, there's an issue with the axle as well, and it's going to take the wheelwright a few hours to repair it."

"Another delay." Brehm frowned. "There is much to be done and little time left." He sighed and drank his small beer, thoughts of Lucy and difficult negotiations swirling through his mind.

Chapter 13

To Join Together

The coach pulled in front of the Dewey Inn after dark, well past the hour when most locals would still be at the tavern. A bitter wind whipped around the building, lashing at their faces, as Johnson and Brehm helped the coachman unload their trunks.

After arranging for two rooms, Brehm and the Johnsons stepped into the sparsely occupied, dimly lit tavern. In one corner, three Green Mountain Rangers sat drinking. The British officers and Adelaide settled at a table against the far wall, away from the rangers. Though the rangers eyed them warily, they made no overt moves and spoke quietly. Brehm recommended chicken pot pie and biscuits. While they ordered, one of the rangers donned his jacket, casting a fleeting glance at the trio as he slipped outside. The barmaid served ale while they waited for their supper.

Returning a short time later, the barmaid brought their pot pies along with a basket of biscuits. Adelaide dug her fork through the crust, releasing a stream of steam. After letting it cool a moment, she took a bite. "Tasty," she said, savoring the buttery flavor. "It's a wonder you didn't grow plump here if all of their food is this good."

The tavern door swung open, and a blast of cold air rushed in, along with a man silhouetted against the moonlight. "Captain Brehm!

I didn't expect to see the likes of you back here. And with guests too."

Brehm turned to the door at the sound of his name. "Mr. Allen!" He waved Ethan over.

"Mr. Allen, this is Captain Johnson and his wife." He turned to the Johnsons. "Captain Johnson, Mrs. Johnson, this is Mr. Ethan Allen."

"It's a pleasure to meet you," Johnson said, shaking his hand. "I've heard a lot about you. And I've met other members of your family. Please join us." He motioned to the table.

Ethan removed his coat, draping it on another bench as he sat. He glared at Brehm. "I'm going to be direct here: Ira told me our delegation was run out of Quebec without even gaining an audience with the governor—or you." Brehm shifted his weight on the bench and bit his lip.

"Please understand, Mr. Allen, there is a certain protocol that must be observed with the governor general." Brehm stiffened, forcing himself to keep his emotions in check. "I had limited authority under those circumstances."

Ethan eyed him carefully. "And now?"

"I carry with me a proposal for peace and security."

"For whom?"

"All of us. Vermont and the crown."

Ethan leaned closer to Brehm, gesturing with his chin in the rangers' direction. "You know, they wanted you arrested. Probably still do."

"I don't blame them. These are tense times," Brehm replied. "Of course, you'd probably have another set of clients if they did."

Ethan considered Brehm for a moment, then formed the slightest of smiles. Brehm visibly relaxed as Ethan broke into a hearty laugh. "So, you heard about the trial?"

"Not from the source. Care to elaborate on what happened?"

By the time they'd finished dinner, Ethan had promised to get word to the council.

The men were exchanging their goodbyes when Adelaide spoke. "Mr. Allen, I'd like to see Mrs. Armistead tomorrow while you are all in conference. Would that be possible?"

"I don't see why not, though she's back at her place a way out of town. You'll need to follow the Old Church Road for about a mile, and then you'll come across a white stone house on the right. That'll be Lucy's place."

"Thank you kindly, Mr. Allen. Good night."

Ethan left the tavern, glancing over his shoulder as he exited, off to find his brother and plan for the next day.

Brehm looked at Johnson after Ethan's departure. "And so it begins."

<hr />

The next morning, Adelaide walked to Lucy's home, her footsteps crunching atop a thin layer of snow that sparkled in the morning sunlight. The white stone house was surrounded by a low fieldstone wall; smoke curled from one of the two chimneys. As she approached the front door, Adelaide could hear the clanging of some pots or kettles. She had just raised her hand to knock on the door when the door opened. Lucy appeared, dustbin and brush in hand, ready to toss the collected dirt out the door.

"Oh, my! I'm so sorry. I didn't expect anyone—Adelaide!" Lucy stood frozen, her mouth agape. "What? How?" She quickly looked around for Adelaide's companions. "I don't understand."

Adelaide moved in for a hug before realizing that Lucy still held her dustpan and brush. "Oh, I'm so sorry. Let me help you."

"I've got it. I was just cleaning." Lucy stepped around Adelaide and tossed the contents of the dustpan outside. "Come in, please." Once inside, Lucy gave her a tight hug. "How is it that you're here? And alone? Oh my, I have so many questions. Please, take your coat off and have a seat."

The two women sat in rush-bottomed chairs near the hearth, which had several logs crackling and a pot hanging above the fire on a swivel cast iron crane. The room was cozy but not warm, and filled with the yeasty aroma of fresh bread.

Adelaide smiled. "I wanted to come along with Robert and Theodore."

"They're here?" Lucy started to get up.

Adelaide gestured for Lucy to stay seated. "Not here. But in Bennington."

"W...Why? When?"

"We arrived last night. Robert and Theodore are here to see your council with a new peace proposal."

Lucy bit her lip. "I'm happy to hear that, really I am." She cast her eyes to the fire. "I was determined to move on." She fell quiet. Adelaide reached out and touched the back of her hand, and they sat in silence momentarily. "He hurt me so, Adelaide. I don't think I want to see him again," Lucy said haltingly.

"I understand," Adelaide said softly. "But I know he wants to see you. I know he thinks about you all the time." Lucy felt a flutter of emotion as she thought of Brehm. Adelaide reached into her bodice and pulled out a handkerchief, which she handed to Lucy. Lucy dabbed her eyes. "He was eager to come on this mission because of you."

"But he wouldn't even see me in Quebec!" Her throat tightened.

"I know. I think he wanted to but couldn't. Robert told me he argued with the governor general on behalf of reaching an agreement. But the governor was steadfast... until he wasn't. I don't know what changed his mind about sending them here."

Lucy stared at the fire and listened to its sizzling. "I don't know, Adelaide. I don't know if I can suffer any more misfortunes and still go on."

Adelaide watched Lucy's profile, her jaw as she clenched and unclenched her teeth. "Are you willing to give up even taking a chance?" The question seemed more like a plea.

"I don't know. This is so unexpected."

Adelaide sat quietly with Lucy for a few minutes, then reached into her bag. "Let me make you some tea. I brought you some from Quebec." She smiled and got up. "Where is your kettle? And the well?"

Lucy rose. "There's water in the pot there." She pointed to the pot hanging on a swivel arm in the fireplace. "It should be warm enough for tea."

Adelaide retrieved the kettle and filled it with some loose tea leaves from the tin. While Lucy retrieved two mugs, Adelaide ladled warm water into the kettle, replacing the lid, allowing it to steep. As they worked together, this familiar process seemed to restore Lucy's composure. The two women settled into conversation. Adelaide filled Lucy in on her trip and told her how much she hated sea travel. Lucy enjoyed the afternoon respite from her cleaning.

"I should get back to town before dark," Adelaide said. "How about if you join me?"

"I don't know, Adelaide. I'm not ready. I think I would rather stay here."

Adelaide frowned but nodded. "I understand. Can I visit again tomorrow?"

"Oh, yes, please do."

Adelaide glanced at the dust bin and broom leaning against the wall. "Perhaps I can help you organize this place."

Lucy smiled. "I would appreciate it. It's been a long time since I've been here."

The two women hugged their goodbyes, and Adelaide started off for town. Lucy watched her through the window until she was out of sight, leaving only footprints in the snow. The thought of seeing Brehm again thrilled her and scared her, as she caught herself between being vulnerable to hurt yet again and the possibility of happiness. *Perhaps*, she thought.

❦

Ira Allen poked at the crackling logs in the fireplace of his parlor adjusting them. General Warner, the baron, and du Ponceau gathered there after supper. Ira returned to his wingback chair, joining the others with his glass of claret. They were discussing the progress of negotiations.

Warner took a sip of his wine. "We're close, gentlemen, damn close. Captain Brehm today proposed recognition for our republic in exchange for a military alliance." He smiled, remembering the moment. "I almost leaped out of my chair in elation, but I restrained myself." He swirled his glass, watching the rich burgundy color cling to the

sides. "We need to squeeze more than just recognition out of them."
He looked at the baron. "We demanded the waterways on our borders
and through British territory remain free to use. The Connecticut
River, Lake Champlain, and the Hudson River are the lifeblood for
Vermont. We don't want Yorkers blocking their use."

"Independence in exchange for a military alliance." The baron nodded his head in contemplation.

"You were a key in this," Warner continued, addressing von
Steuben. "I believe Brehm recognizes how you've made our rangers
into an effective fighting force with tactical superiority."

"And yet they could overwhelm us in numbers come spring," Ira
said. "What's in it for them? There's more to this. There has to be."

"Addition by subtraction," the baron said as Ira returned a quizzical
look. "They free up their forces from fighting us and can redeploy
them against the French. Plus, they have Vermont as a peaceful ally,
one they can call on for help if their restless French population ever
decides they'd rather not be under British rule."

Ira nodded and raised his glass of claret in a salute to von Steuben.
"You may just be right."

"Tomorrow we'll be steadfast in our terms. I can't see Captain
Brehm scuttling an agreement because of that. The captains may desire
this agreement more than we."

Later that evening, Baron von Steuben and Pierre du Ponceau, each
with a mug of ale, sat in the deserted Dewey Tavern. Azor lay sleeping
on the wooden floor next to the baron's feet. Shadows danced on the
walls from the flickering candlelight of the lantern on the table and the
dying embers from the stone fireplace. The two were the last patrons
still there.

The baron took a draft of his ale. "Think about everything we've accomplished since we wandered into this very tavern." He smiled and stretched his back, raising his arms. We're on the verge of gaining recognition of our independence. Maybe not the independence we dreamed of on our travels to this continent, but a great achievement nonetheless." He allowed a thin smile as he contemplated the earlier conversation.

"Based on General Warner's assessment, I anticipate they reach an agreement quickly," du Ponceau said, then fell quiet in contemplation. "And when they do, Friedrich..." He traced the pattern on the mug with his forefinger, unwilling to meet the baron's eyes. He had already decided, but his words felt heavier than anticipated. "And when they do, I'm going to leave," he said softly.

The baron began to object, but du Ponceau looked at him and held up his hand for him to remain silent. "I've thought about this, Friedrich. Paris was a vast city, and I could find exciting people to spend time with. Even Boston had interesting diversions if you knew where to look. But this? There's no privacy here. And not enough people. I cannot stay."

The baron glanced at the sleeping Azor. A thousand thoughts rushed through his mind: the fire almost reaching the supply of gunpowder aboard the ship that brought them across the Atlantic; his joining the Continental Army in Boston only to be unceremoniously expelled when his and Pierre's relationship was discovered; how tenderly Pierre took care of him after he was shot in battle. Pierre was always there for him. "But what will I do without you?" he whispered. "I need you with me."

"This is why I've been pushing for you to learn English. Maybe now—"

"I can, but not well, Pierre," the baron said in English. "I prefer *Deutsch*."

"I knew you understood more than you were letting on," du Ponceau said, smiling. He looked at his pocket watch. "We should get going."

The baron stood, and Azor arose, watching his master. The baron and du Ponceau walked across to the exit, the creak of the wooden floor echoing in the empty room. The baron walked with a limp but carried his cane. "Where will you go?" the baron asked.

"Philadelphia. But not until spring, when the traveling is easier."

He placed his arm around Pierre's shoulder as they ventured into the cold night.

The night chill stabbed Brehm through his wool blanket as he lay awake, Egbert Benson's words from the shadows echoing in his head. He shifted positions and adjusted the blanket. *Strike a deal, the governor said, a military alliance. Warner is open to that. But Benson's whispers, the French, can I trust it? Perhaps delay an accord. Investigate for any French involvement. No! An agreement is in our best interest. And in Lucy's best interest as well.* With the thought of Lucy, images of her danced in his mind, the light catching the green and gold flecks in her eyes, her laugh. *I must see her again and set things right once we reach an agreement.* He drifted off to sleep but woke with a start, a cold sweat drenching him and his heart racing. The fading image from a dream: of Lucy turning her back on him, as he had done to her, and slipping away. He calmed his breathing but couldn't fall back asleep.

Morning came much too early. He dressed and met the Johnsons for breakfast. They sat in the corner of the almost empty tavern, the rising sun bathing the interior with golden rays. The fireplace was already roaring, fighting off the chill of the night.

Brehm wrinkled his nose at the smell of the coffee in his mug but took a gulp of it nonetheless, wincing at the bitter taste. "That's horrible," Brehm mumbled, taking another sip.

"Robert," Brehm leaned closer as he whispered, "I've been thinking about the council's demand allowing free use of the waterways. The most important item is gaining the military alliance. That's what Governor Haldimand wants. How about we agree to their demand in return for their guarantee that they will not block the use of waterways by the British or our colonies and provinces. Additionally, they need to allow us right-of-way for movement of troops through the Vermont Republic."

"It's an equitable exchange," Johnson replied. "Though they may balk at allowing troops on their soil."

Brehm stroked his chin, nodding. "If we're to have a military alliance, it must include free movement."

"Their General Warner seemed to warm to the idea as you went through the provisions," Johnson said quietly.

The barmaid came over to bring their meals, and they changed their conversation topic. After breakfast, Brehm and Johnson walked to the council meeting room.

———— ✦ ————

At the sound of hoofbeats approaching, Lucy peered out the window. Silhouetted against the late afternoon sun, two riders dismounted.

Lucy watched them come into view from the far sides of their horses.

"That's the baron! And Mr. du Ponceau," Lucy said to Adelaide, who was stirring a cast iron pot of soup above the fire. "What could they want here?" She opened her door as they hitched their horses.

"General, Mr. du Ponceau, this is unexpected," Lucy said. "Please come in."

"*Frau* Armistead, it is a pleasure to see you again," the baron said in English. Du Ponceau smiled behind him.

"I have a guest." Lucy turned to Adelaide. "May I present Mrs. Johnson, Captain Johnson's wife." The baron reached for Adelaide's hand and brushed a kiss against it while du Ponceau gave a slight bow.

"Frau Johnson, your *ehemann* asked that I see you back to Bennington," the baron said.

"Husband, he means," du Ponceau said.

"Ach, *ja*. Husband."

"Is there a problem? Did something happen?" she asked, her voice etched with concern.

"No. I have a note from him," the baron said, switching to German to speak faster. Du Ponceau translated as he spoke. The baron pulled a note from his pocket and handed it to Adelaide, who snatched it from his hands.

The fire sizzled and hissed as her eyes scanned her husband's writing. She smiled wide. "They've reached an agreement," she said. Then she looked at Lucy, "including recognition of the Vermont Republic."

Lucy stood stunned, her hand covered her mouth. Adelaide hugged her. "I can't believe it," Lucy gasped.

"Frau Johnson, your presence is requested for a celebration tonight," the baron said. "Mr. Allen asked that you also come, Frau

Armistead."

"Oh, do come with!" Adelaide said.

"I don't know." Lucy turned away. She imagined seeing Brehm. *I don't want to see Theodore; I'm still angry with him.* "I don't think I should."

Adelaide stepped over to her. "It'll be fine. I'll be there for you," she said quietly.

"Adelaide, I don't think I'm ready. I can't."

Adelaide's smile faltered briefly before she said, "I understand," and hugged her again. "But I need to go. I promise I'll see you tomorrow if you'll have me."

"Oh, yes. I'd like to hear all about it."

Du Ponceau offered Adelaide a ride back to town, which she accepted, and the three of them left Lucy's home. Lucy watched them ride off, her heart divided between dashing after them and remaining.

───◆───

A fire roared in the fireplace, casting a gentle warmth as the guests gathered in the Vermont Council's second-floor meeting room, starkly contrasting the bitter wind outside. The windows were swathed with forest green and deep blue bunting. Cast-iron sconces, each with a pair of candles, dotted the walls, while a twenty-four-candle tin chandelier hung above. The aroma of molasses, spices, and rum wafted through the room from the warm flip punch. A murmur from the early arrivals filled the room. The invited guests included the council members, General Warner, Baron von Steuben, Bennington notables, and their wives.

Ira and Ethan Allen stood on one side of the room, away from the fireplace, Ira with a mug of flip, Ethan with ale. They spoke in a hushed voice. "He said Lucy didn't want to attend this evening," Ira said, recalling du Ponceau's words after his return with Captain Brehm's wife. Ira frowned and shook his head. "I should have ridden there myself."

"You were busy; there was no time," Ethan replied. "Tomorrow morning, we'll ride there and make sure she's here for the signing ceremony. She should be here to see our republic recognized by Great Britain."

"You know as well as I why she's not here," Ira said, glancing at the door as they awaited the British officers' arrival.

"Captain Brehm asked me about Lucy earlier when we had a few minutes privately," Ethan confided. Ira's nose wrinkled at that. "I know your misgivings about him, and I wasn't with you in Quebec, but I think he's an honorable man. If there's a chance that he can make Lucy happy, I'd like to see her take that chance."

A murmur rose from the room's far end, causing the brothers to peer in that direction. Captain Brehm, Captain Johnson, and Adelaide entered the room. Brehm scanned the room but was quickly surrounded by the crowd. He shook every hand offered with a reserved smile. This contrasted with Johnson, with his broad smile and vigorous handshaking. Adelaide hardly managed to stay with her husband. Ira watched the spectacle with a bit of envy. *Will my role in all this be remembered? The travel to Quebec City, the long days—and nights—of negotiation. Would we have achieved all this without me?* And then another thought flashed into his mind: *Would we have achieved all this without Lucy? And Brehm's enchantment with her? Or the baron, for that matter, stumbling into this very building less than a year ago?*

Ira was lost in thought when he was jostled. "Captain Brehm, it's a pleasure to see you this evening." They shook hands.

Ethan shook his hand as well. "Captain Johnson, Mrs. Johnson," he greeted as they stepped beside Brehm.

"I was just thinking, I'm happy we're able to host this event," Ira said. His face grew stern. "Though if you had hosted us in Quebec, we may have been able to celebrate sooner."

"We all have superiors who must be respected," Brehm replied. "Your appearance in Quebec was unexpected, and I could not free up my time, having recently returned."

"Spoken like an officer," Ethan interjected. He turned to the Johnsons. "Captain, Mrs. Johnson, may I get you something to drink?"

"I think we'll make our own way over there ourselves and leave you with your brother." Johnson smiled.

Ethan, a bit disappointed, turned back to Brehm and Ira. "Many months of hard work—on both sides—have led us here."

Brehm nodded. "And I'm gratified to be a slight part of it."

Ira raised his eyebrows. "A slight part? Returning with terms advantageous to both parties was key. I'd venture that your superiors will be pleased."

"Then the delay was providential," Brehm replied.

Another murmur rose from near the entrance, along with a few shouts of "huzzah" as General Warner and Baron von Steuben entered, each formally attired in a Green Mountain Rangers officer's uniform. With du Ponceau at his side as always, the baron ambled, attempting to hide his limp as he greeted the assembled.

Brehm watched as they entered. "I am looking forward to in-depth strategy discussions with them," he said, nodding in their direction.

"Our intercourse today on the details of our military alliance was, shall we say, informative." *I was apprehensive that their stance excluding militia and loyalist troops movement through Vermont would scuttle the agreement. But I believe their wariness of New York is justified given their recent history. And if Benson was telling the truth, I'm distrustful myself.*

"If you'll excuse us," Johnson said. Taking his wife's arm, he led her to the drinks table. Brehm nodded to Ira and Ethan and followed the Johnsons.

"Ever the gentleman, even when you verbally started to spar," Ethan said to Ira. "Just remember, the agreement isn't signed and sealed yet. I would suggest you rest the sparring until after noon tomorrow."

Suddenly Ira looked past his brother. "Look," he mouthed. Ethan turned around. Standing at the door was Lucy, wearing a full-length twilight-blue wool coat. Ethan jerked his head around and searched for Brehm. He found him at the opposite end of the room. He had also noticed Lucy's entrance.

Brehm was focused on Lucy. His mouth was dry, and his heart beat loudly in his ears. *She's here! Adelaide said she wasn't coming this evening, but there she is! She's more beautiful than I remember.* A swell of shame and guilt at having left her surged over him. *I should have gone to her in Quebec.* The room seemed to freeze in time as if all that existed was Lucy. *I missed her more than I realized.*

Adelaide watched as Brehm stood rooted, unblinking, at the sight of Lucy. "Captain, go to her; she's waited long enough," she said softly. Brehm heard the words as if they came from some distant, ephemeral place.

But Brehm stood still, his legs heavy, unwilling to move. *What if she isn't here to see me?*

As he watched, Lucy removed her coat, revealing the ivory floral-print dress with a crimson petticoat he had purchased for her at Madame Roux's. That sight broke his spell. A hand on his back nudged him toward her, and his legs began to move.

Lucy spotted him and watched as he slowly walked toward her. *How can it be that I was so angry at him, but now, seeing him, that all dissipates? All the hurt he caused me, I have no desire to bring up to him anymore. How could I ever remain cross with him?* She remained standing, her eyes locked on his, as she smiled.

He reached her, took a deep breath, and opened his mouth to speak. Only a hoarse "Mrs. Armistead" escaped in not more than a whisper. Lucy held her hand out, and Brehm instinctively brushed her knuckles against his lips. The feel of her hand in his, its softness, and the gentle perfume of orange blossom on her skin grounded him in the present moment. "Mrs. Armistead," he said again, but still in a whisper. "What a pleasure it is to see you again. I still love that dress on you."

Lucy blushed, and her attention shifted behind him. "I believe you have some associates with you this time."

Brehm, focused on Lucy, suddenly became conscious again that there were other people in the room. The faraway look in his eyes disappeared, and he swallowed hard. "Of course," he gestured to Johnson. "Mrs. Armistead, may I present Captain Johnson, and you already know his wife."

Captain Johnson kissed the back of Lucy's hand. Adelaide hugged Lucy and whispered, "I'm so happy you're here."

Lucy turned to Brehm. "I've missed our games of chess, Captain, as I'm still not skilled enough to beat Ethan," she teased.

"I look forward to demonstrating my improved skills then."

Brehm and Lucy gazed at each other. While they allowed silence between them, their eyes spoke volumes. After a moment, Brehm asked, "Mrs. Armistead, may I escort you to get something to drink?" He hooked his arm through hers and escorted her away, leaving Johnson and Adelaide. As they watched them walk away, Ira and Ethan Allen stepped over.

"It is almost as if they hadn't been separated these three months," Ethan said. He turned to Captain Johnson. "I look forward to the official signing ceremony tomorrow, Captain. And I definitely look forward to shaking the hand of a new ally at that time."

Johnson laughed and slapped Ethan on the back. "Something we all are looking forward to." Johnson glanced at Baron von Steuben laughing with some members of the council. "I sense that your baron is an astute military intellect. I hope I have the chance to hear of his experiences in Europe."

The baron's many tales flashed through Ira's mind. "He does enjoy retelling those stories, especially over a drink or two!"

The celebrants enjoyed the evening. The official signing ceremony was set to take place at Noon the next day.

——————◦◦◦——————

I'm glad I stayed at Ira's after last night's celebration, Lucy thought as she stirred the coffee she was heating over the fire. *Though I think I'd rather have gone home with Theodore.* She smiled to herself.

"You're looking quite happy this morning," Ira said, entering the room.

"I was just thinking, I'm glad I decided to attend the celebration last night."

"I am as well." Ira beamed at his sister. "You're attending the signing ceremony, aren't you?"

"I wouldn't miss it. We've worked too hard for so long. And lost a lot of good people along the way." A momentary pang at the loss of her husband washed over her.

Ira recognized her look. "They won't soon be forgotten. We owe a debt of credit to them." He placed an arm around her shoulder. "We owe you as well." She reached up and patted his hand in thanks.

"After breakfast, I'm going to borrow your wagon," she said. "I need to get home and dress for the ceremony."

Several hours later, the Allen brothers entered the inn. The room had been cleared of tables except two at the far end near the fireplace. One was covered in a forest-green baize tablecloth, the other in red baize matching the St. George cross of the Union Jack. A single red candle burned on each table, along with a quill and inkwell. Jonas Fay, selected by the council to officiate the ceremony, was already there when the Allens arrived. He wore his powdered wig and finest suit: a slate gray wool frock coat reaching his knees, a sage-colored waistcoat, and ivory wool breeches.

Fay greeted them enthusiastically and admitted to Ethan, "I'm not sure we'd be here today if you hadn't won the Yorkers' case."

"Justice prevailed," Ethan responded. "The council did the right thing."

Baron von Steuben arrived along with General Warner, and they made their way over to the Allen brothers. "We've made much progress since I walked into this tavern almost a year ago," the baron said in English. "I confess I had my doubts about this when we first spoke.

Vermonters are *mutig*." Ira cocked his head at the word.

"Brave?" ventured Warner.

"*Ja,* brave," von Steuben nodded.

Warner laughed. "So help me, I think I've learned some German."

"Where is Mr. du Ponceau?" Ira asked. "I didn't think you two could be separated."

"Delayed," von Steuben answered, avoiding Ira's gaze and looking toward the tables, his voice carrying a tinge of melancholy. "Is everything ready?"

"Dr. Fay has two copies of the document," Ira replied. "He and Captain Brehm will sign both. Captain Brehm will take one copy back to his superiors."

"Come spring, we'll provide a company of rangers north of Lake Champlain, along the border, with the intent of joint activities with British units from Montreal," Warner said. "General von Steuben will have command of the collaboration with our new allies."

More people wandered into the meeting room, stymieing any additional discussion about the agreement. Lucy entered with du Ponceau. She stopped to speak with a few of the women already there while du Ponceau strode toward the baron and took his customary place by his side without saying a word.

A hum of anticipation arose as Captains Brehm and Johnson entered in immaculate regimentals, followed by Mrs. Johnson. Lucy, standing nearby, greeted Adelaide. The captains were too mobbed for her to do anything more than catch Brehm's eye and smile. Brehm and Johnson made their way slowly through the throng of well-wishers to the front of the room, shaking hands and chatting. They exchanged greetings with Warner and von Steuben, Ira Allen, and Jonas Fay.

Ethan had already stepped aside to the right of the tables and was standing with Lucy and Adelaide.

Fay stood behind the tables and raised his hand, holding it up until the room quieted. "To the good people of the Vermont Republic, I welcome you." Cheers and huzzahs rang out. Fay raised his hand again. "This is an auspicious day in the history of our republic. We are here to formalize our agreement with the crown's representatives, Captains Brehm and Johnson, in which they officially recognize our independence!" More cheers erupted. "We enter an alliance with our new friends from the British Empire, a mutual defense pact that ensures the security of our borders, peaceful relations with our neighbors—all of them—and free access to our shared waterways for trade." More cheers. "I invite Captain Brehm to speak if he so wishes." He stretched out his arm to Brehm and gave a slight bow.

Brehm waited for the murmur to subside. "Friends—and I am grateful to call you friends—there were times during our extended negotiations that I despaired that this day would come. Persistence and compromise have succeeded, whereas before, there was wariness and apprehension." *With some deceit from Governor Jay, it would seem, that forced Haldimand's hand*, Brehm thought. *Will it hold?* "This day, the seventeenth day of December 1778, the Vermont Republic stands alone no more." The room burst into applause. As the shouts settled, Brehm turned to Fay. "Let's make this official."

They took their seats at the tables, the British officers at the red baize, Ira Allen and Jonas Fay at the other. Another member of the council placed copies of the agreement before the signers. The men signed the copies before them, exchanged copies, and countersigned. The loudest sound in the room was the scratching of the quills against the papers. Brehm took a burning candle and dripped wax next to his signature. When enough had gathered, he took out the governor general's seal matrix and pressed it into the wax. Fay did the same with his document. They exchanged papers once again and repeated the process. The men stood, shook hands, and held the documents for the crowd to see. The assembled erupted in celebration. Brehm glanced at Lucy. Tears of joy streamed down her cheeks.

⸺◆⸺

Ethan Allen invited a small gathering of people to his home the evening after the official signing of the Bennington Accords, as the agreement was commonly known. Guests were gathered in the morning room, to the right of the center hall, which Ethan used for informal entertaining. He had taken out bottles of rum and brandy, a ceramic jug of mulled wine, and a cask of mead to celebrate. The candles in the chandelier and sconces cast the room in an amber light. A fire raged in the single fireplace along the back wall, warming the dozing Azor and the other visitors as the last rays of the sun peeked through the windows.

The baron and du Ponceau spoke rapidly together in German, while Ethan and Brehm huddled together as well. Amid his conversation with Adelaide, Lucy, Ira, and General Warner, Johnson glanced at the chattering baron and du Ponceau. "I look forward to interacting with the baron. I've worked with Hessians before."

"Don't call him a Hessian." Warner laughed, almost spitting out his drink. "He despises that. He's Prussian, but I'd say he's a thorough Vermonter now." He nodded his head with pride as he looked over at him. "As you work with him, I know you'll be impressed with his skills,

Captain Johnson."

"I look forward to it," Johnson replied.

"General von Steuben," Warner called out. "Come join us."

The baron and du Ponceau joined the conversation. While the men were talking, Lucy caught Adelaide's eye and ever-so-slightly tilted her head toward Ethan and Brehm, wondering what they were huddling privately about. Then she watched as they stepped into the parlor, on the opposite side of the center hall, Ethan was nodding his head as Brehm spoke. She kept glancing over then looking away to avoid being caught staring. Suddenly, Ethan stepped into the center hall and scanned the morning room, spotted Ira, and called him over to join them. Lucy's curiosity piqued.

"What do you think?" Lucy murmured to Adelade.

Adelaide shrugged. "I've been around so many muted military conversations, I've taught myself not to get my hopes up about knowing what those conversations are about."

Lucy and Adelaide watched the three men as they spoke. Finally, Ethan smiled wide, slapped Brehm on the shoulder, and shook his hand. Ira said something and shook Brehm's hand as Ethan looked at his sister. Lucy averted her gaze.

"What was that about?" Lucy whispered.

"We'll likely never know," Adelaide replied. "I'd like more wine. Come with me."

Lucy was about to pour more mead for herself when she spotted Ethan's chess set on the bookshelf, where it had been moved out of the way for the gathering. She smiled as she saw it. *I can't wait to play Theodore again. Maybe now that the agreement is done, he'll have time.* Then she shuddered at a sudden thought. *Perhaps now that the deal is done, he'll leave!* She touched Adelaide's arm. "Adelaide, do you know when you're returning to Quebec?"

"Are you that eager to have us gone?" Adelaide laughed.

"No, no. Just the opposite. I was hoping we'd have more time."

"I haven't heard." Adelaide gazed behind Lucy. "But here's someone who might know."

"Mrs. Armistead." Lucy turned to face Brehm. "I was wondering," he hesitated, shifting his weight from this right foot to his left. "I was wondering if I could speak privately with you in the parlor?"

Lucy looked at Adelaide. "Go," Adelaide mouthed.

"I, well, I was about to partake in some mead," Lucy stammered.

"I promise I'll get you some after," Brehm said softly. "It'll only take a moment."

She nodded and followed Brehm into the parlor. Once there, he positioned himself to speak privately, his back to those in the morning room. He faced her, his hand fumbling in his pocket. "Mrs. Armistead, when I first was given the mission of attaining peace with Vermont, I never could have imagined the dramatic turns that journey would set me upon. It was a political mission, and we have succeeded in those efforts. I'm even happier with the outcome, having become familiar with many people here, especially you. I need to apologize for running out on you. I don't have any excuses for that. I hope you can forgive me." His eyes pleaded.

"Captain, I could never remain angry at you. I'm happy you returned."

Brehm smiled at her, fumbled in his regimental pocket, and pulled something out. "I was hoping you felt that way. Having left you before, I don't think I could bear leaving you again." He held out his arm and opened his palm. The candlelight danced on the surface of a golden ring. "I love you, Lucy. Will you marry me?"

Lucy felt breathless, and her hands trembled at the unexpected proposal. She heard Brehm speaking through the cloud of her thoughts: "You now know Vermont is secure in her independency, and though my duties take me back to Quebec, we can build our future together."

I do love him. But what about my home here? Vermont has always been my home. Could I leave it all behind? "Yes. Yes!" Lucy jumped into his arms and hugged him. When she let go of him, he took her hand and slipped the ring onto her finger.

"I want you by my side always, Lucy," Brehm whispered. "I need you."

"You make me so happy, Theodore." Her eyes glistened with unshed tears.

There were cheers and clapping from those in the other room. Brehm faced them, a flush rising in his cheeks. "I hadn't planned to make this a public event. But I'm certainly happy that the people I'm closest to are here." Lucy moved beside him.

"A toast!" Ethan shouted.

"Wait! Wait!" Brehm shouted back. He held Lucy's hand and led her through their friends, stopping to pour Lucy a mug of mead and a brandy for himself.

Ethan held a glass as they gathered in a semicircle around the newly engaged couple. "I hadn't expected to be making a toast of this sort this evening, but I could not be happier about it. Lucy, I was not always around for you, as I was a guest of friends of the captain." He nodded and smiled at Brehm. "He played no small role in my returning home and has proved himself an honorable man. I am thankful that Lucy has found the courage to love again. She deserves it." He turned to Brehm. "Captain Brehm, I think by now you understand the Vermont spirit. You're a lucky man. I know you will join together in building a future for yourselves and this new alliance between the crown and Vermont." He lifted his glass. "To the captain and my dear sister! May your love for each other be as strong as our love for this land and as steadfast as the resolve you've shown for our countries." He swallowed the contents of his glass to shouts of "Huzzah."

Brehm put his arm around Lucy's shoulder and held her tight. "I'll be proud to call him brother," he whispered.

Baron von Steuben stepped forward, du Ponceau at his side. "Friends." Azor sat up at the sound of the baron's voice and watched him. "I am proud to call myself a Green Mountain Ranger."

General Warner raised his glass to the baron and shouted, "Proud to have you."

"Captain Brehm, we both have known war," the baron continued. "But the bond of peace is what builds the future. In uniting your life with *Frau* Armistead, you do not just join two *herzen*."

"Hearts," du Ponceau interjected.

"Hearts. You also demonstrate the hopes of Vermont and the trust of the crown. May your life together shine as bright as this new friendship between Vermont and the empire!"

"Hear, hear," Johnson shouted, raising his glass.

"Enough," Brehm said, holding his hand up for them to stop.

"Oh no," Adelaide said. "Not before I make a toast for my friends." She smiled at Lucy. "Though I've only known Lucy briefly, she's been like a sister to me." A vision of his lost sister flashed to Brehm's mind. "From the darkest times to this moment of joy, Lucy has shown the courage that few possess." She locked her arm in her husband's. "And now, to see her with our good friend, I think fate has brought you two together. Captain Brehm, you have seen the field of battle, but the battle for Mrs. Armistead's affections was your bravest fight and by no means an easy one." She looked at everyone gathered. "Lucy, you have also fought many battles, just not in the field. Now it is time for you to find peace, and I couldn't be happier that you've found it with our friend." She raised her glass.

"That's enough toasts," Brehm said, holding his hand up again. "I can't help but feel that this is the culmination of everything I've worked for these many months. I wish for nothing more than the friendships we've fostered here to extend between the peoples of Vermont, Quebec, and the British Empire. With Lucy by my side, I know anything is possible. But tonight, we celebrate how fortunate I am." His friends closed in around them.

Adelaide held Lucy's hand and admired the ring. "I had no idea he brought that with him," she told Lucy. "I am ecstatic you'll be in Quebec City with me."

Am I really leaving Vermont? My family? She gazed at Theodore. *My home is with him now.* Lucy smiled.

Brehm gazed into her eyes, mesmerized by the way the candlelight danced in them, and smiled back. *Would any of this have happened without Lucy? Surely she inspired the very idea of the accords.* And now, with her by his side, he was content, knowing that no matter what happened next, peace and happiness had finally found him.

Epilogue

Baron von Steuben sat at his desk reading the correspondence just delivered. Azor rested by his feet. The summer breeze wafted through the open windows of his home. His 400-acre homestead, located in the foothills of the Green Mountains north of Bennington, had been awarded to him by the Vermont Council for meritorious service to the republic. *If only Pierre were here with me to enjoy it, walking these pastoral grounds we could never have imagined in Europe. Well, let's see what he's been up to.* He opened the wax seal and read Pierre's letter.

12 June 1780

My Dearest Friedrich,

Affection, gratitude, and every motive that can weigh on the feeling mind induce me to write you a letter. Philadelphia is a wondrous city, bustling with commerce and ships from around the world! What a fortuitous meeting with the young Benjamin Chew last summer when I arrived. He was keen to introduce me to his sister, Maggie, who is intelligent and interesting. Still, as you can imagine, nothing moved forward. His introductions to society did help me gain employment with the British military, translating Spanish, French, and German. I have started a collection of books, adopted from a retired clergyman, and add to it at every opportunity.

He read the rest of the letter. *Pierre is doing well; I am happy for him.* He picked up the second letter, from the recently promoted Major Brehm.

24 June 1780, Quebec City

General von Steuben,

It is with great pleasure that I write to you about the birth of our child, Ethan Friedrich, who was born last week. We could not ask for better friends than his namesakes. Your leadership on and off the field cannot be overstated. The boy is healthy and doing well. Lucy sends her love. We look forward to your next visit to Quebec.

The letter went on to speak about Lucy, the strength of the alliance, and his hopes for the future. Von Steuben placed the letter back on his desk, sat back, and smiled. *Stumbling into Bennington was the best decision I never made.*

Cast of Characters

Vermont Republic

Seth Warner - Brigadier General, Vermont Republic commanding officer

Baron Friedrich Wilhelm von Steuben - Prussian General; Vermont Republic Inspector General

Azor - von Steuben's faithful Italian Greyhound

Pierre Etienne Du Ponceau - Interpreter for Baron von Steuben

Ira Allen - Diplomat

Ethan Allen - Ira Allen's brother

Lucy Armistead - Ira Allen's sister, widow of Elias

Jonas Fay - Physician, member of the Vermont Council

Samuel Fairbanks - Lieutenant Colonel, Green Mountain Ranger

Elijah West - Owner, Windsor Tavern; Captain, Green Mountain Ranger

Elias Armistead - Green Mountain Ranger

Nathaniel Reed - Green Mountain Ranger

Jacob Thomas - Green Mountain Ranger

British Empire

Frederick Haldimand - Governor-General of Canada

Theodore Brehm - Captain, aide-de-camp for Frederick Haldimand

Robert Johnson - Captain

Adelaide Johnson - wife of Robert Johnson

Guy Bell - Major General, Indian agent for Mohawk and Iroquoi

New York

John Jay - Governor of NY Province

Caleb Griffith - Lieutenant, Physician, NY militia

Egbert Benson - NY Attorney General

Allen Billingsley - Colonel, NY militia

Henry Hawkins - NY jailor

Joseph Turner

Acknowledgements

I would like to thank friends and family members who read early versions of my manuscript and offered valuable advice. Their feedback helped me make improvements and confirmed I had a story worth telling. My editor and cousin Sherry Chiger once again did a masterful job of editing and pointing out areas where my text could be improved—or cut entirely. Her comments have not only improved this book but also enhanced my writing skills. I am also grateful for the support of my family, who often asked, "Are you done yet?"

I've used standard American English spelling throughout the novel. Though in speech, I've attempted to add a flavor of the 18th century. For the created letters, I've stuck more closely to 18th-century language. However, I've modified it to make it more understandable to the modern reader. Any errors in the text or my use of period language are strictly my own.

Afterword

My original idea for a follow-up novel to For Our Cause Was Just was to have a book made up of several novellas or novelettes exploring various characters and areas set in the aftermath of the Continental defeat in the American Revolution. This particular story was intended to focus on Baron von Steuben and Pierre du Ponceau after the baron's dismissal from the Continental Army. As this story evolved, I realized its deep connection to the story of the Vermont Republic itself. As I developed this concept, it grew into a full novel. I still intend to tell those other stories in future books.

Vermonters were constantly engaged in border skirmishes with New York over disputed jurisdiction of the territory, as well as battling Indian raids sponsored by the British. Also at this time, the revolution's outcome remained uncertain. Beginning in 1779 in our timeline, Ethan and Ira Allen conducted secret negotiations with Governor Frederick Haldimand on establishing Vermont as a separate British province as part of Canada. While there is some debate on whether this was a ploy on the Vermonters' part to spur Congress to admit Vermont as a state or sincere negotiations, they were ultimately cut short after the British surrender at Yorktown. These negotiations are commonly known as the Haldimand Affair.

While researching the Haldimand Affair and uprisings of the era, it became clear that Vermont could not succeed in gaining independence by military means in an armed uprising. Aside from the American Revolution, uprisings against British rule in the 18th and early 19th centuries—from Ireland's 1798 Rebellion to various colonial revolts—were crushed by superior British military resources.

So how could Vermont succeed? As I thought about it more, it became clear that victory had to have been aided by some outside force or other circumstances that came into play. The phrase "for the love of a woman" kept floating through my mind. The influence of personal relationships on political negotiations is well-documented historically. A British officer's emotional investment could realistically affect delicate diplomatic proceedings. This romantic element provided a plausible mechanism to influence the negotiations' outcome.

In writing this novel, I consulted numerous articles on The Journal of the American Revolution (https://allthingsliberty.com/) website, as well as their podcasts Dispatches: The Podcast of the Journal of the American Revolution. These are both excellent sources covering the colonial period with many contributing historians. I also consulted the resources of the Vermont History Museum (https://vermonthistory. org/) in Montpelier, VT, which was a great help. Beyond these sources, I examined letters between British military officials and political leaders in England that helped in understanding the political and financial pressures they were facing.

Many of the vignettes contained in here are true—from Samuel Fairbanks's kidnapping to the battle tactics and individual actions to the baron's Azor—though I've changed many of the circumstances under which they occurred.

If you enjoyed this story, I'd be grateful if you could leave a rating and review on Amazon or Goodreads. Reviews help other readers discover alternate history fiction like this.

About the author

Larry Chiger's lifelong fascination with the Revolutionary War comes alive through his role as a loyalist reenactor for the 1st New Jersey Volunteers (https://1njv.org/). A healthcare IT professional by career, Larry has recently channeled his passion for history into storytelling. He lives in the Philadelphia area with his wife, where they enjoy spending time with their family and beloved granddogs.

Also by the author:
For Our Cause Was Just

Visit the author's website:
www.larrychigerauthor.com